HEAT OF THE MOMENT

GEORGIA LECARRE

SOME BOOKS

HEAT OF THE MOMENT

Georgia Le Carre

Heat of The Moment
Published by Georgia Le Carre

AUTHOR'S NOTE

The little town of Bison Ridge doesn't exist... although I do wish it did!

PROLOGUE

TIFFANY

https://www.youtube.com/watch?v=8tEoGjSQpes

I opened my front door to find Tiffany, my stepsister standing outside. A bit of a surprise since I hadn't seen her in more than three months. Her pouty lips seemed more bee-stung than ever, and her hair was an even whiter shade of platinum. She was wearing pearls and a pretty blue dress that made her eyes look almost turquoise.

Right off the bat I should say, we don't get along, so I wasn't all that happy to see her.

"Hello. Aren't you going to let me in?" she purred.

Wordlessly, I opened the door wider and stood back. She walked through in a cloud of exotic perfume and made her way to my couch, where she perched on the edge of it as if she was afraid it would soil her clearly expensive dress.

"Where's your dog?" she asked, looking around her warily.

"At the dog groomers," I said.

She visibly relaxed. As she should. Pogo hated her with a passion. He snarled, growled, and snapped whenever she got within an arm's length of him.

"Do you want something to drink?" I asked.

"Perrier with a slice of lemon, please."

My lips twisted. Tiffany never failed to amaze me. She really thought the whole world existed only to serve her. "I don't have Perrier. You can have a glass of tap water if you want," I offered, even though I had bottled water in the fridge.

Her nose wrinkled. "I'll pass." She flashed a fake smile and patted the space on the sofa next to her. "Come sit with me."

I suppressed a shudder at the thought of being that close to her. Now it was my turn to be wary. "What's up, Tiffany?"

"Nothing. I just wanted to talk to you... to tell you something."

I moved to the sofa, but sat away from her. "Tell me what?"

She took a deep breath. "Okay. It'll be best if I just come out and say it."

"Go on then."

"Steven and I are in love."

For a quick moment, I thought I'd heard wrong, because the words she said didn't make sense. Unless... unless by some weird coincidence it was a different Steven. "Steven?" I echoed.

"Your Steven," she confirmed artlessly.

The shock was incredible. Never in my life had I felt so utterly shocked. Steven and her! Even the idea made me sick to my stomach. "What?" I blurted out.

Tears pooled in her big blue eyes and spilled down her beautiful face. She always could turn on the tears as if they were on a tap. She opened her purse and pulled out a tissue.

"We didn't mean for it to happen," she sobbed, as she carefully dabbed her cheeks. "It just did. You have to believe me."

"What a little bitch you are. You stole my boyfriend, and you didn't mean for it to happen?" I think I was still in shock or disbelief because my voice sounded strangely calm compared to her dramatic crying and sniffing.

She blinked with surprise. It was very rare that I was ever confrontational or horrible to her. From the time we were children, I learned, it was better to let Tiffany have her way. That way my stepmom wouldn't complain to my dad, and my poor dad wouldn't have to stand up for me and be trapped in fierce arguments about how he spoiled me. This was followed by the silent treatment that lasted for days on end and made my stepmother resent me even more even though outwardly she played the 'how lucky Willow is to have such a nice and caring stepmother' part to perfection.

Tiffany, for her part, very quickly understood she could walk all over me with no consequences. And walk all over me she did until the day my dad died, then I took a step back from my whole family, and reduced my interaction with her to a strictly necessary level.

Until now.

Unbelievable. She was unbelievable. First, she helped herself to my boyfriend, then she invited herself to my home to give me the news.

A malicious, almost cunning look came into Tiffany's suddenly dry eyes. She tossed her head and her long white-blonde curls bounced on her shoulders. "I don't know why you're being so mean about it. Steven and I tried hard to resist the attraction, but we simply couldn't. We fell madly in love with each other. It's not like what you had with Steven. Steven told me the two of you were just fucking around."

My eyes widened. Wow! Just fucking around!

Oh, the bastard! *That* was what he thought we were doing for the last two years. The coward didn't even come to tell me himself. He left Tiffany to do his dirty work. Typical.

Tiffany was staring at me curiously, intensely, as if she was actually drinking in my pain. The betrayal was like a knife in my chest, the pain sharp, but I took a deep breath. No matter how much it hurt I would not give Tiffany the satisfaction of knowing just how much she had hurt me.

Keeping my face expressionless I looked back at her. Then without warning something clicked in my head, and suddenly, I was nine years old again and we were both standing in my bedroom. She was laughing cruelly and holding out my favorite blue blouse with the colorful dogs on it. It was ripped. She had ripped it right in the middle.

And now, here she was, in all her bottle-blonde glory, at it again. She simply couldn't bear for me to have anything she didn't, not even the cheap blouse my mom had given to me before she died. And here she was again, holding out my ripped relationship... just because she couldn't bear for me to have anything she didn't.

But things were very different now. My beloved dad was gone forever. I didn't need to protect him anymore. I forced the most confident smile I could muster on to my lips.

"The only person Steven Harriman loves is Steven Harriman, and you're either stupid or deluded for imagining you'll be anything more to him than I was." I threw my head back and laughed. It sounded a bit crazy, but it was a real laugh, because it was true. He was as narcissistic as she was. She had finally met her match. They deserved each other.

"I'll prove how wrong you are. You'll see," Tiffany promised heatedly.

I stopped laughing and stared at her. Her eyes were glittering with a strange light and her fingers were clawed as if she wanted to scratch my eyes out. I finally understood what I had never comprehended before. She was jealous of me. She always had been. Why, when she was the beautiful, loved one, I would never know.

Shocked by the intense hatred and insane rage, I'd glimpsed in her eyes, I jumped to my feet. I couldn't wait for her to get out of my sight. I never wanted to see her again.

"Get out," I snarled.

"With pleasure," she cooed. The mask was back on her face. There was a satisfied smile on her face as she stood, then looked around my small apartment dismissively. "You should invest in some air freshener. The whole place of stinks of dog. Ugh. How can anyone live like this?"

"Get out," I screamed.

Satisfied she had inflicted maximum pain on her victim, she sauntered out of my home, her head held high.

1

WILLOW

THREE MONTHS LATER

"I'm so sorry to have to tell you this, Willow, but Tiff and Steven are getting married," Olivia, my half-sister informed gently. Her voice was full of pity.

I clamped my free hand over my mouth to stop any sounds. Thank God we were on the phone, and she couldn't see my reaction. My knees suddenly felt like jelly and I quickly sat down. The taste of failure filled my mouth. All kinds of thoughts filtered into my mind unchecked.

Crazy, angry, negative thoughts.

I was wrong when I predicted their relationship would not work out. They seemed so different. He was commitment shy. She was hopelessly flighty. Based on her past behavior, I assumed she would break it off once the novelty of taking what was not hers wore off. She didn't want my blue blouse; she just didn't want me to have it.

It was just a matter of time.

But even in my worst nightmares, I'd never thought it would get this far. Tiffany had won again. She had proved me wrong and showed me that she could get and keep my man. They were actually getting married!

Still, to be fair, why wouldn't she keep him? He was a good catch. Great career prospects, handsome in a boyish way, and there was something else that was very important to her. He came from a good family. A well-to-do family.

It hit me then that he must really want her too.

Steven and I were together for two years and marriage had never come into the conversation. He never even hinted of wanting it. His career came first. Everything was always about him.

With hindsight, I guess, I should have seen this coming when he left his high-powered job and moved to our small town in Wisconsin. I'd laughed when I heard that, thinking he wouldn't last. Steven loved the city. There was no way he was going to last more than six months there.

I'd even imagined the scenario where he came knocking on my door and begged me to take him back. Telling me he did not realize how selfish she was. How she wouldn't lift a finger to do any housework, how she always wanted to be waited on. In my head, I saw myself tell him to go fly a kite. Not only did I have my pride to consider, I could also never trust him again. The joke was on me. Instead of begging me to take him back, he was getting married to Tiffany.

So, there they were, the two most selfish people I knew, out there happily making plans for their wedding while I sat here in my tiny apartment alone.

My shoulders slumped.

My personal life was in a shambles. After what Steven and Tiffany did, I left Bison Ridge, and everything that was familiar to me and moved to New York City where I was still finding it hard to make friends. My neighbors preferred a nod and a distant smile to anything real, and I was still too raw to actually go out and make new friends. Hearing that Tiffany was getting married made my nonexistent social life seem even more pathetic.

"Willow? Are you still there?" Olivia asked. A note of worry had crept into her voice.

"When is the wedding?" I croaked.

"Er... in eight weeks." In my mind's eye I could see her wincing as she said it.

"January? Tiffany is getting married in the dead of winter?" I noted, surprised. For as long as I could remember she had always planned a spring wedding for herself.

They must be in a hurry to get hitched. I really read them both completely wrong. Tears filled my eyes and I quickly wiped them off with the back of my hand. I hated that even now they could still hurt me.

"Willow darling, are you okay?" Olivia asked.

"Yes, of course," I replied immediately, even though I was clearly not okay. Not by a long shot. I felt mortally wounded. As if I was a small animal in the woods and someone had thrown a spear at me, and now it was stuck in my side.

I gripped the phone tighter and gritted my teeth. I was not a loser and I was not going to let my family see my pain. My whole family had all taken Tiffany's side. Had my father been alive, he would not have tolerated that kind of behavior in his family. Dad had been the fairest man I'd ever known.

Tiffany would have been the outcast, not I. After I left, the family had embraced them both, even though they all knew she had stolen him from me. A wave of grief came over me, almost knocking me over, as a deep longing for my father swept over me.

"Um... one more thing..." Olivia trailed.

"What?" I asked, dreading her answer.

Olivia hesitated for a couple of seconds. "Tiff is pregnant."

I thought of petite, glamorously skinny, snake-hipped Tiffany and for a few seconds, I couldn't even imagine her pregnant, but it sure explained the January wedding.

"Poor thing suffers from terrible morning sickness," Olivia mumbled into the bruised silence.

I was the oldest, my father's child, Tiffany was my step-mother's child from another marriage, the spoiled one who got her way all the time, and Olivia was the youngest, the child who belonged to both parents. Consequently, she took their love as a given as she never had to win favors from either parent. That made her confident of her place in the world and she became the one who tried to make everyone happy. She was doing it now too.

"Of course, Tiffany suffers terribly," I muttered bitterly." Tiffany can't get a cough without thinking it's lung cancer."

"Yes, she can be a bit of a drama queen," Olivia agreed with a small awkward laugh. There was another uncomfortable silence before she rushed into it with what was obviously a prepared pitch. "Um... are you going to come for the wedding? Obviously, we'd all love you to come, but you don't have to. I mean, no one would blame you if you didn't. It could be awkward and really difficult for you. Why should you put yourself through the pain of watching Tiffany marry your ex-boyfriend—"

"I'll be there," I cut in firmly.

"Willow—"

"It's fine, Olivia," I interrupted in a weirdly crisp voice. "It won't be difficult for me at all. To tell the truth Steven is a narcissist. We would eventually have broken up anyway, and I'm actually quite happy he's found someone who suits him better."

"Really?" Olivia asks doubtfully.

"Yes, really. To be perfectly honest, I've moved on and even met a nice guy. While its early days, things are looking promising," I babbled on while a part of me stood aside and watched incredulously at the brazen lies that were flying out of my mouth.

"Oh! You already met someone new?"

"Yes," I squawked. My whole body felt hot with guilt.

"Well, that's really great news, Willow. I'm so happy for you. I'll tell everyone at home. They'll be so relieved. We've been worried you might still be broken-hearted. Family gatherings have not been the same without you." She paused for a second, then said the words that made my head spin. "I know... why don't you bring your new man along to the wedding?"

"Okay, I will," I heard myself say calmly, but my eyes were squeezed shut with horror at the mess I'd dug myself into.

"Fantastic. Can't wait to meet him. What's his name?"

"Look, I've got to go. Someone's at the door. I'll talk to you soon, okay?" I said, and quickly cut the connection.

2

WILLOW

https://www.youtube.com/watch?v=esWu36l3vY8

With Pogo hot on my heels I hurried to the kitchen. I stood at the window and stared out of it. My cheeks were burning. Did Olivia really believe me? She could be a bit naïve, but Tiffany or my stepmother would never believe it.

The view from the kitchen had been the selling point of this tiny apartment. If you crane your neck out of the window on a good day you get a partial view of Brooklyn Bridge.

A scream filled the air.

At first, it sounded as if it was coming from the apartment above. Pogo gave a frightened yelp and ran off to cower in a corner. I sank down on the cold, tiled floor and began to sob. Pogo came out of his hiding spot and tried to get into my lap. He made strange growly noises of confusion and distress. It was not his fault. Poor baby. I stroked his silky head.

"It's okay, it's okay," I soothed, again and again, like a monotonous mantra. I didn't know if I was saying it to calm him or myself. But it helped us both.

Pogo started to relax. He draped his small fat body over my thigh and let out a sigh of contentment. If I knew Tiffany at all, for sure the wedding would be a lavish affair at the country club where all the crème de la crème of society weddings were held. The easiest thing would be to make up an excuse of being ill and not attend the damn thing, but I was not going to give her and Steven the satisfaction of hiding away.

I could see Tiffany crowing to Steven, "See, I told you she was lying. She hasn't found a man at all, and now she's too embarrassed to show her face."

And they would both imagine I was still hurting over their betrayal.

No, I had to show everyone I'd moved on. I was happy. I didn't need Steven. Which was the God honest truth. I was well over Steven. In fact, I was eternally glad I didn't waste another second with him. Two years was enough. The thought of them getting married didn't really hurt that much. I could go to that wedding no problem. The thing that hurt the most was my family's treachery. The way they had all taken Tiffany's side and turned their backs on me, abandoned me as if I was the one who had done the unspeakable thing, not her.

I sighed heavily.

If only I had not told Olivia I'd found someone new.

But I had, which meant I now had to bring a date. Where the hell was I going to get a date from? There was my friend, Emma's brother. He was pretty good looking and a nice guy to boot.

I chewed my bottom lip. No, that wouldn't work. I told Olivia I'd found someone new in the city.

No, I needed a brand-new suitor, someone who would make Tiffany rethink the idea that she'd gotten the better of me. It came to me like a lightbulb. I could hire an out of work actor to be my date for the wedding.

But paying someone was risky. My family was inquisitive and one little mistake on his part and they would know it was all a sham. My stepmother was like a ferret for gossip and rumors. And the humiliation that would bring would be intolerable. I could already imagine the delight in Tiffany's eyes. It would be the best present I could ever give her.

No, I would just get on one of those online dating sites. If that didn't work, maybe, I could hang out in some of the trendier bars in town.

How hard could it be to find someone respectable in such a big city?

I decided there and then I was going to attend that wedding with my head held high, and a wonderful new boyfriend on my arm, and afterwards, I was never going back to my sleepy hometown ever again. Once this was over, I wanted to stay as far away from my family as I could.

Feeling greatly cheered, I scooped Pogo into my arms and went to pour myself a glass of wine.

I buried my nose in his soft neck and breathed deeply. I loved him so, so, so much. Pogo turned his head and licked my cheek. "You were right about her all along, my darling. She's a manipulative grade A bitch. And all that strong perfume she wears day and night has killed off her sense of smell. You don't stink. If fact, you smell heavenly," I told him as cold wine splashed into my glass.

Pogo made an almost cat-like purring sound at the back of his throat. He was happy, and I had my drink and my brilliant plan.

The crisis, I was certain, had been averted.

3

WILLOW

Seven Weeks Later

https://www.youtube.com/watch?v=bWcASV2seyo

Except it hadn't.

Turned out the meme going round was true: good boyfriends were not so easy to find. Hanging out in the trending bars had yielded nothing. Not that I hadn't been hit on. I had, but they were mostly assholes looking for a quick hook-up.

And after my latest conversation with Olivia where I got the distinct impression that both my stepmother and Tiffany didn't believe I'd actually found a man, I decided that my date for the wedding had to be above reproach. Handsome. Sexy. Successful. A man who would make Steven look like a wet-behind-the-ears boy.

But time was running out and I was starting to panic. I was not going to find such a legend, especially since there was hardly a week left before the wedding. Not that I was ready to give up the search, but I was starting to get more than a little despondent.

As I got ready for the company's yearly party, the temptation to skip it and spend the time curled up on my couch was huge, but I squared my shoulders with determination. No, I needed to go out. Maybe what I really needed to do was get talking with some of my colleagues. Maybe they would know someone who could help.

"We need a new strategy, Pogo." He was lazing on the bed, staring at me as I slipped into a black dress. "Clearly I'm not going to get a date through the conventional ways, so I must think outside the box."

Pogo yawned.

I tried on several outfits, not quite achieving the look I wanted. The bed was a mess of discarded gear. Eventually, I turned to the red dress. It was too slutty for an office party, but what the hell.

I adjusted the long sleeves of the dress. They were the only respectable thing about it. Was it too sexy for an office party? There was a lot of leg on show.

I took a couple of steps towards the mirror. Nah, it was not too sexy, not really. Yes, the dress was short and it clung to me like a second skin, but I was in the big city now. Nobody cared about what anybody else was doing. Anyway, some of the girls at work came to work dressed as if they were going directly to a party afterwards.

If my stepmother could see me, she would definitely have said I looked like a whore. We were brought up to clutch pearls and show as little skin as possible, but I wasn't living in Bison Ridge anymore. I was in the Big Apple, home of the daring and the brave.

My stepmother had no control over me anymore. I would never again let her shame me into behaving in a way that she approved of.

I applied a layer of cherry lip gloss, kissed Pogo, and left.

THE PARTY WAS a disastrous waste of time.

I knew very few people so I stood in a corner, clutching my fifth glass of bubbly, and pretended to admire the Christmas tree left over from the Christmas party as everyone else laughed, danced, and generally had a good time.

A familiar song blasted from the speakers, pulling me from my introspection. Draining my glass, I popped it onto a ledge, and began swaying to the beat. That was when I realized just how sloshed I had become. I decided to go to the restrooms and splash some cool water over my face.

I left the big hall, walked into the corridor and slammed into a brick wall, well it felt like one, but it had warm, strong hands that curled around my forearms and kept me upright.

Shaken, I lifted my eyes all the way up, and stared into the face of a hot, I mean, like magazine-cover hot man. He was easily the sexiest man I'd ever seen in my entire life, and that was even counting magazines and movies. God! His eyes, they were piercing blue.

They robbed me of all thoughts except one. *This here, was exactly the kind of man I was looking for to take to the wedding, and fate had delivered me right into his hands.*

"Whoa! What's the hurry?" the utterly gorgeous beast drawled, his voice dripping with amusement.

4

REX

HTTPS://WWW.YOUTUBE.COM/WATCH?V=VX2U5UUU3DE

"Are you single?" she asked breathlessly, staring at me with a dazed expression.

"Guilty," I admitted, stepping away from her warm curves, and watching her closely. I didn't know what to make of her.

She had the obligatory long blonde hair that I usually went for in a woman, but she was not exactly my type. There was too much intelligence and warmth lurking in those enormous bottle green eyes. I preferred my women blonde and dumb... Still, something about her intrigued and fascinated me. Probably those fantastically long silky legs. I could already see myself opening them and tasting her. That was surprising in itself, since I couldn't remember the last time I'd reacted so viscerally to a woman.

"Oh good," she said, a slight slur to her voice, "because I have a proposition for you."

My eyebrows rose. Well, well... She didn't look like that type, but these days, you never knew.

"Oh no! No, nothing like that. This does not involve sex. Not at all," she gasped quickly.

Pity.

"Come with me and I'll explain," she said, and started to walk away.

For an instant, I thought about walking in the opposite direction. She was clearly tipsy, and I wasn't exactly in the mood for a tanked-up woman, but that thought was gone in an instant, when the sway of her hips mesmerized me. I was staring at her firm round bottom and her long, long legs when she looked over her shoulder, and asked in an almost melancholic voice, "Aren't you coming?"

That must have been what the song of the siren was like for those unfortunate sailors.

Almost against my better judgement I followed her. She led me into a deserted canteen and gestured for me to take a seat at the closest table. I leaned a hip at the edge of it and regarded her. The bright, white LED lighting made her appear almost unreal.

"Would you like a bottle of water or something?" she offered, jerking her head in the direction of some fridges at the other end of the room.

I shook my head.

"I supposed I could snag us a glass of champagne from the party, but I think I might have had too much already," she mused aloud.

"I'm alright for a drink," I said quietly.

She smiled sunnily and it lit up her whole face. Yes, there definitely was too much intelligence and warmth in those eyes.

"I haven't seen you around before. Which department do you work in?"

"I'm... er... visiting from a different branch of the organization," I replied evasively.

"Oh! You're not based here. Which branch?"

"You had a proposition for me..." I reminded pointedly.

She licked her lips, a suddenly nervous gesture, and to my astonishment, my cock jerked to life.

"How do you feel about a weekend trip to Wisconsin, all expenses paid?" she blurted out with what was obviously false bravado.

I kept my face straight. "All expenses paid, huh?"

"All expenses paid," she agreed, nodding eagerly. "In fact, I will even pay you for your time."

Curiouser and curiouser. I rubbed my chin thoughtfully. "Pay me for my time? Just how much are we talking about?"

She had obviously not thought about it until now, because she frowned, then pulled a figure out of the air and let it hang between us, almost breathlessly waiting to see my reaction to her announcement. "A thousand dollars," she blurted out.

"A thousand dollars?" I repeated softly.

A thousand dollars? What a laugh, but how cute of her. I nodded slowly and pretended to be impressed by her announcement.

The relief in her posture was unmistakable. "And if it all goes well, I'm even prepared to double the figure."

Somewhere between the time she said 'all expenses paid' to 'I'm even prepared to double the figure', I had started to enjoy myself. Nothing like this ever happened in my life. All I ever did was crunch numbers so that I could then use the information to wrestle chunks of bloody meat out of the mouths of emotionless sharks. Could I really take a whole weekend off?

Of course, I could.

I just never did.

Until now.

"And what would I have to do in return?" I asked casually.

One thing for sure. She was a terrible actress. She slapped her forehead in a dramatic, over the top gesture. "What's wrong with me? I didn't tell you, did I? Well, you'll be very pleased to hear you won't have to do anything much in return. In fact, hardly anything."

I raised my eyebrows.

She stopped to swallow audibly, then flashed another big, bright smile at me. "You'll just have to pretend to be... my new boyfriend."

Now *that*, I did not expect. I stared at her curiously. "You want to pay me to pretend to be your boyfriend?"

"Well, I know it sounds a bit weird, but it's not. Really, it's not. You see, my stepsister stole my boyfriend and now she's marrying him... and I just need someone to go with me to the wedding, you know, to show them all that I'm not broken-hearted or anything like that, and then I saw you, and I thought you'd be absolutely perfect, so I stupidly thought you wou "

Midway, her voice broke, and tears began to roll down her cheeks.

"I mean, you look like a straight-up, hardworking guy so you can just consider it a weekend away. A free, no strings attached treat that you probably deserve. You really should take the deal. It's a good one. I would if I were you. You'll be staying at a really lovely hotel. It overlooks a lake, and even though it'll be frozen this time of the year, you could go for long walks around it. It's so beautiful around the Lake Club, it'll be almost like walking into a postcard."

More tears ran down her cheeks as she continued babbling, so fast her words tripped over each other.

"And they make the best margaritas at the main bar. I promise you; you won't regret going with me. We'll have to share a suite, of course, but I'll be busy all day and you'll hardly know I'm there. In fact, you won't have to spend much time with me at all. Except during the wedding, of course. And that'll only last for a couple of hours. We don't even have to attend the reception."

The words were still tumbling incoherently out of her, when I pushed myself off the table and walked towards her. Casually, I curled a lock of her blonde hair between my fingers.

She was so startled she stopped talking and went as still as a statue.

The air between us stilled, became pregnant with... something. Her eyes widened and her lips parted. Then, completely unexpectedly, something happened deep in my gut. That place where the first warning of danger usually came from. It was different this time though. This was not a warning. This was a craving. A craving so deep it actually throbbed with life and intensity.

Pretty insane!

My finger grazed her wet cheek and a spark of electricity shot through me. Hell, I hadn't had such a reaction to a woman in a very, very fucking long time. Perhaps because I had designed my life in such a way that all my sexual interactions with women were meaningless, casual, and deliberately impermanent.

I released the lock of hair and stepped back. "The best Margaritas, huh?"

"The absolute best," she whispered hoarsely.

"So... a frozen lake and walking trails are on offer?"

"Totally. I'll even throw in a basket of the most delicious dark chocolate muffins from the local bakery. I swear they are to die for. You could never get enough of Mrs. Sherman's cakes."

"Hmmm... I am rather partial to dark chocolate, but... will I have to be nice to the bitch, though?"

A startled expression crossed her eyes, then a tremulous smile trembled onto her lips. A little giggle she couldn't contain slipped out. "Nope, being nice to Tiffany is not included in the deal. However, you will get bonus points if you don't fall for her manipulative machinations, which all men usually fall headlong into."

I smiled lazily. "Ah, one of those." A female shark. I knew well how to handle them.

A bitter expression crossed her face. "Yes, one of those. She uses her beauty to blind people to her real intentions."

"I'll consider myself warned."

"Good," she said heartily.

The smell of her shampoo was still in my nostrils. Lemon with a twist of something sweet, apricots perhaps. I had an insane desire to bury my face in her hair. "What weekend are we talking about?"

She bit her bottom lip and winced slightly. "This weekend coming."

I stared at her plump mouth. An image of me plunging my cock into it popped into my head. "Kind of short notice, isn't it?"

"I know, but I couldn't find anyone suitable, until tonight when I ran into you."

"Who else besides the bitch will I have to convince?"

"My father died three years ago, so there'll just be my stepmother, Nicole; my half-sister, Olivia; Tiffany, some random family members; and of course, the bridegroom or my unfaithful ex, Steven."

"Whom you're still madly in love with, I suppose..."

Her head jerked back and her voice was hard with disgust. "God, no! He's a selfish, narcissistic, untrustworthy jerk. They deserve each other."

I hid a smile at her outburst. "So why the elaborate charade?"

She seemed suddenly agitated. "Because I did a stupid thing. I told Olivia I'd found someone and things were going well. I only told her that because I didn't want her or anyone else to pity me and think I was still nursing a broken heart, but it backfired when Olivia asked me to bring my new guy along, and now I'm committed to bring someone. Either that, or I'll look like a liar, or even more humiliating, like someone who can't keep any man."

"I see."

"I know it must be impossible for you to understand, but I just want to attend this wedding with my head held high, and once and for all stop the rest of my family from thinking I'm a total loser, or that I'm hurting because I want him back. Also, if I'm honest, I don't want to give Tiffany the satisfaction of thinking she has something I want."

"So, the job description is for me to leave no doubt among your family and friends that I'm head over heels in love with you?"

She clasped her hands and nodded enthusiastically. "Yes."

I should already be in a plane flying back to head office, but being a part of this little adventure was surprisingly entertaining and intriguing.

"Rex Hunter. What's your name?" I asked.

"Willow, Willow Garrett," she replied, and staggered a little. She was more drunk than I originally thought. "So, you *will* do it?"

"Yes. Yes, I think I will," I murmured.

5

WILLOW

"You really mean it? You'll go with me?" I squealed excitedly, part of me still not quite believing he had said yes.

"Sure, why not? I have nothing better to do this weekend, anyway."

"Oh my God! Thank you," I cried breathlessly.

Rex grinned suddenly, and the butterflies in my stomach went crazy. There were no two ways about it. Rex was smoking hot. He had everything I found insanely attractive in a man. Beautiful eyes, a body that clearly saw the inside of a gym a lot, and a slow smile that made my insides swoon.

When his finger grazed my skin something weird happened to me. My breath quickened and my heart started racing like mad. The kind of juvenile reactions I used to have as a teenager when a super cute boy looked at me.

Rex glanced at his watch. "I have to be somewhere else now, but how about dinner tomorrow? We can hammer out our strategy then."

Wow, he was really serious. "Dinner tomorrow sounds great. Thank you so much. I'll pick up the tab."

He frowned slightly, but only said, "Okay. You pick the restaurant then."

"We could go to the Italian at the end of this street. They do an amazing Ossobuco."

"Sure. Seven-thirty good for you?"

"Seven-thirty is perfect," I agreed happily.

"Put my number into your phone and call me if any problems arise."

I fumbled around in my purse, located my phone, and pulled it out. When I had it open, he called out his number, and I put it into my contacts.

"Now give me a missed call," he instructed. The way he issued the command gave me the impression he was used to giving orders, and it made me curious about him.

When I heard his phone ring from inside his jacket, I killed the call.

"See you tomorrow," he said.

Then he was gone.

I stood in the deserted canteen alone, not quite sure if it had all been a dream. Then I looked down at my phone. His number was still there.

I felt as if I had just won the lottery. A lottery called Rex Hunter.

And all that pent up frustration and anxiety came out of me in a rush and I laughed like a demented hyena. No one would feel pity for me with him at the end of my elbow. With a whoop of pure joy, I did a happy dance all around the tables.

Yesssss! I did it. I actually did it! I found a date for the wedding, and what a date I found. I couldn't wait to see the expression on Tiffany's face. This was no blue blouse she could rip into two. She would go green with envy. Rex made Steven look like a boy still in schoolboy shorts.

My best impression of an evil laugh reverberated all around the empty room as I practically skipped and danced my way out of there.

What was even better was that he was from a different branch so after our weekend together I never needed to see him again. Perfect. Just perfect.

Yesssss, Willow. You did it, girl. You did it.

6

WILLOW

Where the devil was I? And why did my head feel like there was a large hammer inside it banging away relentlessly? I cracked one eye open and surveyed my surroundings. I was home in my bed, but the light hurt my eyes, so I shut them immediately. "Owww..."

Yeah, drank too much last night. Suddenly the events of the previous night came to me and I sat bolt upright, both my eyes snapping wide open.

Rex Hunter!

Did that actually happen? I reached for my phone and to my amazement there was a message from him. I opened it:

Table booked at La Chipola 7.30pm. Pls don't be late.

I fell back on the pillow. Ouch, my head. But even so I couldn't stop grinning from ear to ear. A little body jumped onto the bed and started busily burrowing deeper into the covers. I curled my hands around the wriggling body, brought it close to my face, and inhaled the lovely warm animal scent.

"Oh, Pogo," I whispered. "I think I solved all our problems."

He trained his warm chocolate eyes on me and looked pretty happy to hear my news.

"How can you be so beautiful first thing in the morning?" I complained.

He made a small purring sound of pleasure.

"God, how I love you," I cried and pressed his face next to mine.

It was true. I loved him to bits. He was the only living creature that had never disappointed or hurt me. No human being could ever rival him. Well... maybe Rex, but only because he was so damn fine and was about to solve my biggest problem.

My head was too sore for me to lie around in bed, so I got up and trotted off to the bathroom where I proceeded to swallow a couple of aspirins. By the time I brushed my teeth and took a shower, I felt a whole lot better.

I poured myself a mug of freshly brewed coffee, sat down at the kitchen table, and contemplated how I would handle my dinner date. My phone rang; it was Olivia.

"Hey," I greeted cheerfully.

"You sound happy," she remarked.

"I am," I said simply, let her make of that whatever she wanted.

She laughed. "That's good. I always felt bad about what happened between you and Tiffany."

"Don't worry about it, Livy. It's all water under the bridge now," I said airily.

"Anyway, I'm making the name cards for the reception and I realized I still don't know the name of your plus one."

"His name is Rex Hunter."

I hear her scribble the name down, then she says, "Got it. So, how's it going with him?"

"Good. Very good."

"I'm so glad to hear that, Willow. I can't wait to meet him actually."

"Well, you don't have very long to wait."

I heard someone calling her in the background. "Oh, Mom has just arrived. Do you want to say a quick hello?"

"No, no," I said quickly. "I'm just about to go out. I'll see her when I get there."

"All right then. See you at the weekend," she murmured.

"Bye."

With a sigh I ended the call. My relationship with my stepmother was complicated to say the least. This weekend was going to be interesting if nothing else.

Saturdays usually found me in the office, going over stuff I hadn't managed to get done during the week, but today I didn't want to go in. Perhaps it was time for me to go shopping instead. I needed a dress for the wedding.

"I gotta go get myself a dress for the wedding," I said to Pogo.

He nodded solemnly.

I took a cab into town. Paying the driver, I hurried into a little dress shop where I'd, in the past, seen some nice stuff in the window. I was determined to get the classiest dress I could find. It took me the whole afternoon to buy myself two new outfits and a pair of cream shoes. They were all on sale so I was pretty pleased with myself.

Now all I had to do was have dinner with Rex so we could fashion a credible story of our first meeting, etc. etc.

7

WILLOW

I walked into La Chipola at five minutes to seven-thirty. Rex was already seated at a corner table. His dark head was bent to his cellphone. I walked up to the table and said, "Hello you."

He raised his head and smiled at me. Wow! He was even more hunky than I remembered.

"Good. You're on time. Have a seat," he invited cordially.

I'd bought a lot of takeaways from that restaurant so the waitresses knew me well. I could see Isabella surreptitiously pointing at Rex and mouthing, "Wow," while Megan was widening her eyes dramatically to show her surprise and approval at my taste in men.

I nodded a greeting at them and quickly sat down. Bella arrived at our table.

"Something to drink?" Rex asked, taking a sip of his drink.

I smiled at Bella. "Just some water, please."

When she was gone, I opened my purse and pulled out the check I had written for a thousand dollars.

"Here is your first payment and the other one I'll write at the end of the weekend," I said, and pushed it along the table towards him.

He looked at it and frowned. Immediately, I wondered if I had quoted a different figure last night.

"That is what we agreed on, isn't it?" I asked anxiously.

He looked up at me, his mouth quirking. "Yes, of course." He took the check, folded it in half and slipped it into his jacket.

Bella arrived with a jug of water and filled my glass.

He regarded me curiously. "So, where and how did we meet?"

"We met in the rain. I had gone out to buy a hotdog and you were rushing home from work when we ran into each other. The mustard from the hot dog was splattered all over your shirt and coat. I looked up to apologize and that was it. Love at first sight under our umbrellas."

He looked amused, but said nothing.

"Do you think that's too corny?" I asked.

"No, not at all. What happened after?"

I frowned. "We went back to your place."

His eyes glinted. "Really?"

"No, scrap that. That does sound a bit cheap. Let's go with, we went back to your place, you changed your shirt and we went out to dinner."

"And then?"

"And then we went back to your place."

He laughed then. "How come all the girls I date are not that easy?"

"It was love at first sight!" I protested.

"Where do I live?"

"Uh... in the better part of town."

"Got an area?"

"How about the next street? There are some nice apartment blocks on Melvin Street."

He nodded.

Bella came back to get our orders and we both ordered the ossobuco.

"So, tell me more about you?" he invited.

I spent ten minutes telling him all about me, Pogo, my job; basically, poured out my whole life. "Now tell me about you?"

He shrugged. "I will be everything you tell them I am. You can make it up as you go along. What would you like me to be?"

"Oh."

"What would make Tiffany boil with envy?" he asked.

I took a deep breath. "She would hate it if you were super rich."

"Well, then I'm super rich."

"No," I said slowly. "We couldn't pull that off."

"Why not?"

"She'd see through that in an instant."

His eyebrows rose. "I don't see how."

"I mean, don't rich guys arrive in private planes, wear Gucci, and shower their women in really expensive jewelry and designer gear?"

He leaned back. "Actually, we can arrive in a private plane. One of my good friends is a pilot and he owes me a few favors. As for designer gear, an old friend of mine is a personal shopper and dresser of the super-rich. She has a lot of contacts who wouldn't mind lending us some stuff."

I stared at him, surprised. "You'd do that for me?"

He lifted one shoulder carelessly. "It's actually nothing,

plus I enjoy a challenge. Tiffany *will not* see through our act. Are you free tomorrow evening?"

"Yes," I replied.

He picked his phone off the table, started scrolling through it, found a number and clicked on it. "Nina," he said crisply. "Will you be able to fit a friend in tomorrow evening?" He listened, then said, "Good. I'll text you the address and details later tonight."

"Er... what's going on?" I asked, confused by the way he had taken control of the situation.

"Tomorrow, Nina will be your personal shopper. She will arm you with borrowed designer clothes and jewelry."

"But I already bought a couple of dresses today."

"Keep those for another occasion," he said carelessly.

I blinked. "I... er..."

"Ah, the food is here. Smells wonderful."

8

WILLOW

Nina was something else. She looked at me as if she knew something I didn't, or couldn't figure something about my relationship with Rex, but her professionalism was truly top notch.

"Willow," she said with a smile. "A show stopper is what Rex requested and a show stopper is what you will be. You will make a statement no one will forget in a hurry."

"Okay," I agreed happily.

For the rest of the evening, we visited expensive stores and boutiques that were apparently closed to the public, but had opened their doors specially for her. Women of indeterminate age and beautifully coiffured hair, air-kissed her, and offered us champagne and canapes. I felt quite dizzy with indecision at the vast array of dresses that were laid out for us, but Nina knew exactly what she wanted for me.

"Nope, nope, no, definitely not this color, nope, no, no, NO."

Then finally, she said, "Yes, this one. You have good legs. This is perfect to showcase them and it matches your eyes."

It was a gorgeous long, silk green dress, with a high slit up one thigh and showing a generous amount of cleavage.

"This is really sexy," I murmured. "I love it."

"Try it on," she urged.

I carried it to the changing room, loving the soft, silky feel of the material. I'd never owned anything so fine in my life. Yes, I did earn good money, but I lived a disciplined life and tried not to splurge on clothes. I was building up my nest egg every month so I could afford to buy my own place eventually.

I stripped off my clothes and slipped into the dress. Wow! It looked amazing, better than I could have imagined. I turned this way and that way in front of the mirror, admiring the way the outfit hugged every curve in my body as if it had been specifically sewn for me.

I looked hot, even if I said so myself.

I imagined myself walking into the dinner after the rehearsal, hanging onto Rex's arm. Not one person would remember that the groom had been my boyfriend not too long ago.

I came out of the changing cubicle and both Nina and the store owner nodded with approval.

"Here are the shoes to go with the dress," Nina said.

I slipped into the green shoes she put in front of me. They fit perfectly and gave me three and a half inches more of height. Even to my own eyes my legs looked like they went on forever.

"By the way," Nina said, "my friend is a hairdresser. She could do your hair for you, if you like."

"Uh..."

"It wouldn't cost you anything. She owes Rex a favor."

I stared at her. It seemed as if a lot of people owed Rex a favor.

"Trust me, you won't recognize yourself once she and her makeup artist are done with you."

I smiled. "Why not."

"Fantastic. You'll love what Grace and Holly will do for you," she said and immediately made an appointment for me the next day. I also heard her ask them to give me a manicure and a pedicure.

Afterwards, we went to a few more places and picked up a classy cream suit and matching shoes for the wedding and a few casual outfits for the day. In one of the stores a man on a bike came to drop off some handbags. A lovely black and gold Gucci purse and a beautiful cream Chanel clutch.

"These will go with everything you've chosen," Nina said.

Finally, we visited a jewelry store. We were ushered in and taken up an elevator to an area that was apparently only available to the very rich. I was dazzled by the glass cases full of fabulous jewelry. Nina, with my total approval, picked an exquisite emerald necklace to go with the dress, and some other smaller, but equally stunning pieces to go with the rest of the clothes.

It was already nearly midnight when we came out of the store. We carried nothing with us as everything we had chosen would be sent directly to Rex as he would be responsible for them.

I thanked Nina and she hugged me and wished me luck. Then she asked if I needed a lift home, but I refused. I was not actually very far from my apartment. A walk would do me good as I felt slightly disorientated and light-headed.

Everything that was happening to me seemed too unreal to be true.

Cinderellaish...

Too good to be true.

Almost like a dream. In a dream a cow can morph into a cake, then become a tree. I thought about Rex. What would he morph into? It was all so strange. A man who had access to private planes, the services of women like Nina and her specialized collection of people.

Who was he?

I remembered asking him about himself and the way he had so smoothly deflected the question. It was true that what he was had nothing to do with me or what I had hired him to do, but it was still rather bizarre that he would reveal nothing about himself.

And anyway, why would a man who looked like him be willing to help a total stranger in this way? Very strange, but in the end, who he was had nothing to do with me. I hired him for a fair price, he accepted, and that was that.

I wandered down the street to an all-night café and ordered myself a piece of apple pie and a glass of cold milk. I drank thirstily. After all the alcohol I consumed last night, I was still feeling dehydrated. When the pie arrived, I forked it into my mouth and chewed without interest. The picture over the counter had made it look luscious and tempting, but in fact, it was not very good. The only other customer left and I became the lone person in the café.

What if Rex bailed out on me? I would have to pretend to be sick or something. There was no way in hell I was attending that wedding alone.

Just thinking about it made me shudder.

An old fifties song came on. I should be feeling lonely

and sad, but I didn't. Tiffany had stolen my man and my entire family was pretending she was the victim, but it didn't cut as it did before. No, they could all carry on with their coffee meetings and little Sunday gatherings and pretend to be better than me in their small pond.

I had a different life now. I was making my own way in the big bad city and nothing and no one was going to change that.

FOUR DAYS LATER, I checked Pogo into a nice dog hotel, where I was pleased to note how fearlessly he went on to meet and greet the other four-legged guests. After that all I had to do was wait for the SUV Rex had hired for me to arrive.

Finn, the driver, was a lovely man, but other than chatter about the weather, there was no new information to be had about Rex.

As we made our journey to the airport, it dawned on me that the day I'd dreaded and loathed was finally here, but to my surprise, going back home to Bison Ridge wasn't as terrifying as I'd imagined it would be.

Maybe it was my new hairstyle or the lovely French manicure, but I felt confident I could face Steven and Tiffany without showing any negative emotions.

The SUV drove right up to the plane. While Finn opened the trunk to get my suitcase, I was directed up a short flight of steps into the plane. A pretty flight attendant ushered me in with a cheerful smile.

"Welcome aboard, Miss Garrett. Mr. Hunter is already aboard. If you'd like to follow me, I'll take you to him."

"Thanks," I said looking around me in amazement.

I tried to keep my jaw from dropping to the floor as I stepped into the cabin. Everything looked so clean, new, and expensive. Even the atmosphere reeked of wealth and luxury.

The leather seats were cream finished with fine wood grain paneling, and matched the thick carpet. I had never imagined a day when I would travel like this. Obviously, this was a one off, so don't get too used to it, I reminded myself sternly.

This was Rex's friend's lifestyle, not mine.

Rex was seated at the far end with headphones in his ears and his laptop open. He was dressed casually in a pair of black jeans and a black shirt and, God help me, he looked good enough to eat. I actually experienced breathlessness, as if all the air in the space had been sucked out. Heck, even my toes tingled with some kind of static electricity.

Suddenly, I had the disconcerting sensation that I had gone from the frying pan straight into the blazing inferno. The inferno shut down his laptop, slipped off his headphones, and stared at me, his eyes deliberately and totally expressionless.

9

REX

She was wearing an off-white long coat, a cream turtleneck sweater, a beautifully tailored black mini skirt, woolen tights, and black leather boots that came up to her knees. Her fair hair was feathered around her face and neck and fanned out in soft waves around her shoulders.

The transformation was quite startling.

She was gorgeous before, but she was irresistible now. The only fly in the ointment was the niggling idea that someone who went to all this trouble to attend her ex's wedding must be at least still a little in love with him. Well, it didn't really matter to me. His loss was my find. I'd never been the jealous type. What a woman did when I was not fucking her was not my business. Besides, I was not looking for a serious relationship.

She did a preening twirl, and asked, "Well, am I fine enough to pass for a rich man's plaything?"

"Fine enough to hang off a billionaire's arm," I assured.

"Good," she said, sinking into the seat in front of me.

I took a sharp breath. I was not used to having women disturb me the way she did. Her small skirt had ridden further up her thighs. In my mind she was not wearing those thick warm tights. Her long silky legs were naked, and she was opening them in a wide V to show me her wet pussy. 'Go on, Rex. Eat me,' she invited in my head.

"Is everything okay?" Willow's voice intruded into my fantasy.

I looked up at her and smiled slowly. There was now zero chance I was not going to fuck her before the weekend was out. "Yeah, everything is just fine."

"Can I get you something to drink?" Stacey, the flight attendant asked.

"Orange juice would be nice, thanks," Willow replied with a smile.

Stacey disappeared into the back and Willow turned her attention back to me. "What kind of favor do you have to do to be able to ask all this in return?" She gestured around her with an arm.

"It's not as big a deal as you think. The plane drops me off in Wisconsin and picks someone else up."

She nodded thoughtfully. "Hmmm...I see, but it seems to me like you've called in a lot of favors for this weekend."

I shrugged. "I guess, I just like to win."

She frowned. "Win?"

"Didn't you say you'll double my money if I do a really good job of convincing everyone?"

"Yes. Yes, I did and I will."

I smiled. "Good. Now, do you mind if I respond to some emails?"

10

WILLOW

"Go ahead," I said. "I could use a nap." It wasn't a lie. I hadn't slept well the previous night.

He picked up his phone while I curled up on the luxuriously soft seat and got comfortable. I actually wanted to talk to him. There was so much I wanted to find out about him, but it was probably for the best. I was already too attracted. He was just someone I hired to do a job for me. Nothing more.

Less than fifteen minutes later, we were airborne, and I couldn't help but compare it with the times I flew commercial. It was such a pleasure to travel so sumptuously. What a shame normal people like me couldn't fly like this all the time.

I drifted off to sleep and woke up later to someone gently shaking me. I popped my eyes open and to my surprise, I was in a lying down position and Rex was looking down at me.

"I reclined your seat," he explained as I struggled to sit

up. "We only have an hour to go. I thought you'd like to refresh and maybe have something to eat and drink?"

He looked and sounded so concerned, I had to remind myself that Rex was just someone who liked to win. It didn't mean anything other than the desire to keep in my good books.

"Thank you," I said and excused myself to go to the bathroom.

I looked at my reflection in the mirror. I still wasn't used to my new look. It was surprising how different a change of hairstyle could make. Using the toiletries available, I refreshed myself. There was everything a person could possibly need, including a brush still in its plastic packaging for my hair. I couldn't believe I'd slept for two straight hours. I must have been more tired than I thought.

Back in the cabin, I found an appetizing arrangement of fruit, cheese, and little bites waiting for me.

"Dig in," Rex invited.

"Looks yummy," I said as I sat down. "So, don't forget ours was love at first sight," I reminded, as I popped a strawberry into my mouth.

"I remember," Rex said. "In the rain."

"Under the umbrellas," I added.

"Shouldn't we practice?"

The flight attendant came and took away the empty plate after asking if there was anything else we needed. I shook my head and suddenly wished I had kept in touch with my old friends. It would have been so much fun to tell them about the experience of flying in a private plane.

"Is that a 'yes'?" Rex said, drawing me back to the present.

I laughed. "What are we practicing?"

"Touching. Kissing. Being in love. We have to be convincing," Rex said with a straight face.

I laughed again, but awkwardly. Even the idea of kissing Rex made heat run up my neck. "I'm not sure we ever need to kiss, and as for looking like we're in love, I'm sure we'll manage that when the time comes."

"If you say so," he said too casually.

"I do," I said firmly. "Er... how should we say you came upon all this money then?"

"I own my business."

"Selling what?"

"Something glamorous but too difficult for most people to probe into. How about an investment company?"

"I like that," I agreed, thinking of how green Tiffany would be if she thought I had bagged such a man.

We landed and there was a sleek dark green and silver Maybach S class waiting for us on the tarmac.

"Wow," I said. "Called in another favor?"

"Nope. This one comes with the plane, but I have hired a fast car that should be waiting for us at the hotel," he explained, and began heading towards the driver.

We started out on our one-hour drive to the Lake Club, where I had booked us a suite. The entire land was snow-covered and it was freezing cold, but inside the car it was warm and toasty. I literally sank into the plush seat.

My phone rang and I dug into my handbag to get it. Who on earth could that be? I groaned inwardly when I saw my stepmother's name. I hadn't told her the exact time we were arriving in Wisconsin so her timing was just incredible.

"Hi, Nicole," I said unenthusiastically. I became a different person when I spoke to her or my sisters.

"Hi, Willow. Welcome home," she cooed with her usual saccharine sweetness.

"Thanks," I said automatically.

"You could pretend to be happy about coming home."

What on earth was I doing? I was giving the exact opposite impression of what I had intended to. I was supposed to be over the moon in love and happy. I straightened my posture. "I am happy, very happy, just groggy. I slept the whole way here," I said, injecting some cheer into my voice.

"Oh good. That means you're fresh. Everyone's here, come and say hello."

I gripped my phone tighter. I wasn't ready to see them yet. But if I said no, they would all conclude I was hurting. "Okay. I'll be there."

"You *will* bring your new man with you, won't you?"

I swallowed. What reason could I come up with for saying no. Off the top of my head, I couldn't think of any. Oh dear, I promised Rex he would hardly have to work for his money and already it was looking like a lie.

"Of course, I will," I agreed with fake brightness.

"Where are we going?" Rex asked, when I ended the call.

I shot him an apologetic look. "My stepmother's house. Everyone's there apparently. Sorry."

11

WILLOW

"Don't apologize. That's what we're here for," Rex said evenly.

My hands felt cold and clammy with sheer nerves and anxiety. "What if they see through us, Rex?"

"I don't know about you, but I can put up a damn fine performance when I want to. They will never see through me," Rex declared confidently.

That made me feel a little better. "Okay, I think I'll be able to match you, but coming home has made it all so real. I'm actually going to witness my ex and Tiffany get married. That is so freaking twisted."

An oddly fierce expression had flashed in his eyes while I was speaking, but it was hidden very quickly. I wondered what I had said to cause it.

"If you prefer, we could skip the whole circus and just show up for the wedding?" he suggested mildly.

"Hell no! We've come all this way. I won't chicken out." I smiled weakly. "Besides it's not fair on you. You deserve the chance to double your money."

He smiled back. "Exactly. How about we go to the hotel, freshen up, then take a trip into the lion's den... hmmm?"

I nodded. It really did feel as if we were going into a lion's den. "Yes, freshening up first is a brilliant idea."

The rest of the journey was spent in silence. Me staring out at the snow-covered landscape worrying about how it was all going to turn out, and Rex giving his entire concentration to his laptop.

Eventually, we arrived at Bison Lake Club and I nudged Rex. "We're here. Look. Isn't it marvelous?"

He looked up and gazed at magical scenery around him, then looked into my eyes. "Yes, you were right. It is very beautiful. You ready for Act 1, Scene 1."

I nodded. "You're really serious about this, aren't you."

"I never do anything halfway. Either I'm all in or I'm not in at all."

I smiled at him. "You've just made me feel a thousand times better."

He smiled back, his teeth white and gorgeous against his tanned skin. "Then let's go show them how it's done."

We left the breathtaking scenery and climbed up the hotel's steps. Even through my thick coat I could feel the warmth of his hand on the small of my back. Suddenly, a strange thought popped into my head.

How amazing if this was all real?

I shook my head to clear the thought. It was unworthy of me. The last thing in the world I needed was to get entangled with such a man as Rex Hunter. Not only was he an enigma he was also clearly, completely, and totally outside my league.

A porter greeted us and held the door open before he went out to get our luggage. The inside of the Lake Club was exactly as I remembered it. Quaint, and reminiscent of the English hotels portrayed in old Hollywood movies. The receptionist's desk gleamed with the patina made from decades of wood polish.

"By the way," Rex whispered in my ear. "I cancelled your booking for a deluxe suite and booked the Presidential Suite in my name. I thought it more appropriate since I'm supposed to be the rich guy and you're my new-found love."

"What?" I asked with a frown. How dare he? I remembered the Presidential suite being twice the price of the Deluxe and the Deluxe was already far more than I wanted to pay for a hotel suite.

Suddenly, Rex swooped down and covered my mouth with his. I was too shocked to do anything. His mouth was warm, hard, and insistent. I felt it like an irresistible, searching, plundering force. The flame of desire curled like a snake around me. His aftershave filled my nostrils as my mouth opened instinctively.

He deepened the kiss and I clung to him helplessly because he had become the only solid thing in my dizzy, swirling world. I forgot everything that existed outside the feel of his mouth on mine and the way my heart beat like a wild, mad thing inside my chest. I had never known I could feel like this. Never.

No man had ever done this to me.

As suddenly as it had started, it ended. He tore his mouth away from mine. I was shaking with shock. I didn't want him to see the effect his kiss had on me so I grasped his arm and, looking down, took deep gasping breaths. "Why did you do that?" I asked.

He put his face next to mine and whispered, "Because the town's busybody is walking towards us and instead of telling half the population she saw us arguing, she can tell them about how you've bagged yourself a guy who can't keep his hands off you."

I touched my shaking lips and he looked amused. "I knew we should have practiced the kissing part. You don't surely want the town gossip to see you looking like you wandered into the woods and came across a bear."

"Willow, is that you?"

I was still astounded by the way my body had responded to his kiss, but I composed myself as best I could and turned around to find Mrs. Dearborn standing no more than a foot away from me. Under a blue hat her light blue eyes were wide and shining with avid curiosity.

I forced a smile. "Hello, Mrs. Dearborn."

"Why? Look at you," she exclaimed loudly. "You've become quite the city girl with a new hairstyle, and fancy clothes. I almost didn't recognize you."

"Well, you look just the same."

She patted her neatly brushed hair. "At my age, I'll have to take that as a compliment." Her eyes slid over to Rex. "I heard you'd be coming to the wedding with your new man. Is this him?"

"Yes, this is Rex. Rex, meet Mrs. Dearborn."

"How nice to meet you, Mrs. Dearborn. Willow has told me so much about you."

Mrs. Dearborn's bosom swelled up as she preened with surprise and pleasure. "Has she? All good things I hope."

"Of course," he replied smoothly.

Mrs. Dearborn's eyes slid quickly to me then back to Rex. "Will you two be staying long?"

"Just the weekend, I'm afraid." Rex managed to make his

voice regretful. He really was better at acting than I'd given him credit for.

"Perhaps you could come over for morning coffee or tea tomorrow. Barney would love to meet you, and you can have a piece of my fruit cake. I make the best fruit cake in town. I'm sure Willow—"

"Thanks, Mrs. Dearborn," I interrupted, "but I don't think we'll have the time. The schedule is quite tight as it is."

"Pity. Perhaps next time. Homemade fruit cake is my favorite thing and since yours is the best..." Rex said charmingly.

"Yes, yes, both of you must come next time," she gloated happily, her eyes gazed adoringly at Hunter.

"Goodbye, Mrs. Dearborn," I said stiffly.

"I'll see you both at the wedding then," she said, not making any moves to leave.

"I'll look forward to it," Rex answered suavely, and to my surprise Mrs. Dearborn actually blushed.

"Goodbye, Mrs. Dearborn," I repeated.

"Right then, I better go back to my tea, Marybeth and I were having tea over in the Orangery when I looked out of the window and saw you both arrive so I thought I better come over and say hello. Cheerio until Sunday," she sang, before sailing away in a cloud of perfume.

I watched her for a few seconds before I turned to face Rex. My whole world felt like it had been turned upside down, but he was looking at me as if nothing had changed. As if the kiss had meant nothing to him. He was just an actor, earning his money.

"How did you know she was the town gossip?" I asked.

He grinned. "The hat gave her away."

I smiled. "Well, it was a very good guess."

"Shall we?" he asked, gesturing towards the reception.

I nodded and we walked on in. The receptionist on duty was Jane. I knew her from school days, but we were not close or anything. She was a few years older than me.

"I have a booking under the name of Rex Hunter."

Jane didn't even need to check her computer. She flashed a big smile at both of us. "Of course, Mr. Hunter. Hello, Willow. Nice to see you back. Here for the wedding, huh?"

"Hi, Jane. Yup. Back for the wedding... with my man," I added.

Her eyes returned to Rex, then back to me, and there was a flash of envy in her face.

"Right," she said, then turned her attention to Rex. "Guests of the Presidential suite have their check-ins done in the privacy of their rooms by the concierge. Let me ring him and he'll show you up to your suite."

At that moment I realized Rex was right. True, I was originally annoyed and irritated that he had cancelled my booking and gone for a far more expensive option without asking me first, but I could see now how odd it would have looked if I had been the one who booked and paid for our suite. And if I was truly honest, I now approved of his decision to go for the Presidential suite.

It was exactly what a very rich man would book. If I recollected correctly, it even came with its own butler. That should make Tiffany quite green with envy.

"I'll reimburse you for the cost of the suite," I muttered, as we turned away from Jane.

"You won't have to," Rex replied. "The company will pay for it."

I frowned. "Why would the company pay for it?"

"Because I'm putting this whole weekend down as a working one. Other than the times I'll be pretending to be your devoted, madly in love boyfriend I'll be working flat out."

"Oh, okay."

12

WILLOW

While the concierge checked Rex in, I wandered around the magnificent suite. I had never stayed anywhere so beautiful and opulent in my life. The bathroom was all marble, the main bedroom had the largest bed I'd ever seen in my life, and there was a balcony overlooking the lake.

The view alone was worth the extra cash which I wasn't going to have to pay. The weekend was looking better and better. As soon as the concierge left, the butler came in.

A straight-backed, po-faced, grey-haired man in a black suit. There was a reverential air about him. As if he'd spent all his whole life serving people he considered to be better than himself. He didn't resent the fact, but deemed it a privilege. He introduced himself as Solomon.

Expertly, Solomon opened the bottle of complimentary champagne sitting in a bucket of ice, and carried two flutes of cold bubbles on a silver platter to the nest of sofas we were sitting on.

Standing a few feet away he offered to unpack and steam

the wrinkles out of our clothes. I refused because I was too embarrassed by the idea of him looking through my underwear, but Rex told him to go ahead. When he disappeared into the main bedroom where all the luggage had been taken, Rex turned to me.

He raised his glass to me. "To a successful weekend," he murmured.

"To a successful weekend," I echoed, raising mine to his.

I regarded Rex from over the rim of my glass. That kiss had completely blown me. How desperately I wanted more, and yet after this weekend he would be gone forever from my life. Not once did he mention ever doing anything beyond this weekend. Part of me wanted to sleep with him anyway, but another part of me was terrified to.

Danger signals were going off everywhere. I knew nothing about him. He was deliberately secretive.

A man like him could definitely shatter my heart into a million pieces. The smart thing to do was to leave it alone. Why did I want to further complicate this weekend? It was already going to be hard enough as it was.

"Tell me about your stepmother?" he invited.

"What would you like to know?"

He smiled slowly. "Whatever you would tell your lover, I suppose."

The thought of him as a lover made my skin tingle. *Get a hold of yourself, Willow.* I cleared my throat.

"Well, Nicole owns the biggest beauty salon in town and both my sisters work for her. She's smart, she's ambitious, she's well liked in the community. But we don't get along. We pretend to, of course. We did that for my father's sake and now it's an ingrained habit. It's how we roll. We never argue or disagree about anything. We just pretend all the time to be part of a loving family. Even when there's no one around, we pretend. But secretly, she is furious with me and always has been. She hated the fact that my father and I were a package. She wanted my father, but not me. And any love he showed me, irked her to no end. As a child she always made me feel like an unwanted annoyance. I think she would have loved it if I had contracted some childhood disease and died."

Rex's eyes widened. "Whoa!"

"No, I'm serious, but by the time this weekend is over you'll think I am an evil drama queen portraying her in that way, for you will never see anything but her mask: a loving mother who is so kind and generous she can love a child that is not hers as much as her own. That mask never slips. No, that's not true. It used to, a couple of times at the beginning when we were alone, but not anymore."

Solomon came out of the room holding some folded clothes. "If there is nothing else, Sir, I'll take these to the laundry room to get them done," he said to Rex.

"Thanks, Solomon. By the way, I've hired a car which should already have arrived. Could you get someone to bring it out front for me, and leave the key with the doorman?"

"Most certainly, Sir," Solomon replied with a courteous nod, before he withdrew quietly.

"I have a confession to make," I said softly.

He smiled. "Yeah?"

"Yeah. I was actually very annoyed when you changed my booking from an ordinary deluxe to the Presidential deluxe, but I'm not anymore. This is wonderful. Just the view alone is worth it. It will be an experience I will cherish forever."

He looked at me curiously. "Why didn't you want the Presidential suite? It was necessary for your act and you can afford it."

"Yes, I guess I can afford it, but maybe I thought it was too much for me."

"Too much?" he queried.

"Too luxurious."

He raised an eyebrow. "Too luxurious?"

I shrugged. "I mean, come on, a butler? There are better things I can do with my limited resources."

"Hmmm... have you ever asked yourself why you were never taught about money in school?"

"To be honest the thought never crossed my mind."

"Think about it though. Shouldn't the creation of money, the care and the management of it be an integral and essential part of every child's education?"

I nodded. "I guess so."

"So why isn't it?"

I frowned and shook my head. "I don't know. Why isn't it?"

"Maybe because you are not meant to understand it. If you did, maybe you would not be such a willing slave of the system. Money is not scarce, Willow. Nor is it a limited resource. It is created out of thin air everyday by central banks around the world. The real truth is *nothing* is scarce. Not money, not water, not oil...nothing. In fact, the opposite is true.

"The nature of this world is pure abundance. To know and understand that all you have to do is tend to a garden. Look how fast the weeds grow. You cut them. They grow back. You cut them again... and they grow again. You use pesticides, and a different weed adapts to it and grows there. The cycle never stops."

"The plenty is all around you. Everywhere you look. Sheep never run out of fleece no matter how many times you shear them. Snow can fall without rest for days, weeks, or months if you go higher north. The desert is never-ending sand. The tropics hold a profusion of lifeforms. The abundance is even in us, humans. Our bodies are constantly changing, trillions of cells completely replacing themselves every few years. A woman can give birth every year for many years. But it is us, we, who stop the abundance."

I stared at him. "I've never thought about life like that... and I've never met anyone else who does."

"If you expect scarcity, Willow, that is what you'll get. Look for abundance, expect it, and it will be there for you."

"Okay. I will," I promised.

He glanced at his watch. "Shall we go meet the enemy?"

I stood. "Yeah. Just give me five minutes to freshen up." I looked down at him. "Um... which room do you want?"

"Which room do you want?"

"The smaller one will do me fine."

He looked at me levelly. "Why not the bigger one?"

"Well..."

"Train yourself to look for abundance, Willow," he said softly.

I bit my lip. All my life I'd tried to make everybody else happy. "Okay. I'll take the main bedroom."

He smiled approvingly. "Good. That's my girl. See you in five."

13

REX

"Wow! What a shiny freaking beast," Willow gasped as we neared the bright red car.

"Yup, beauty, huh?"

"What is it?" she asked, in an awed whisper.

"A Mercedes McLaren."

She looked at me, her forehead furrowed. "It must have cost you a lot even to rent it. Surely far more than what you'll earn from me."

I shook my head. "Nope. I love fast cars and I have a running deal with a particular rental company. I pay a fixed monthly fee and they send me the cars that are not rented out. I don't care what type or class of car they send as long as it's fast."

"I see. I hope you're not thinking of driving like a madman on these snowy roads. I've lived in these parts most of my life and I know how treacherous they can be in this weather."

"I race on my days off, so relax," I said.

"Whatever, but I'm not getting into that monster until you promise you'll drive like a normal person."

I laughed and conceded, "Fine. I'll drive like a normal person."

We slipped in and I pressed the start button and the motor instantaneously roared to life.

"Whoa," she yelled at the thunderous noise, and I laughed.

And so, we began the journey to her stepmother's house. I glanced at her. She was a bigger person than I was, that was for sure. There was no fucking way I would attend this wedding if I were in her shoes. And if I did, I'd definitely have to punch someone.

"Nervous?" I asked.

She shook her head. "Not yet."

"Good."

Less than forty minutes later, we drove into the driveway of a sprawling single-story house. It had an appealing wrap-around porch and a low roof.

"Is this where you grew up?" I asked.

"Yes." She looked at me and swallowed hard. "I'm nervous now."

"Don't think you can convince the people in that house you're in love with me?"

"Of course, I can. Don't sweat it, gorgeous," she blurted out, then looked away with embarrassment at her unintended confession. "The real question is, can you?"

"Do you know what I'd like to do right now?"

"No."

"I'd like to open your legs wide and suck your pussy until you scream... and even then, I won't stop. I will suck you for hours and hours until you're so fucking swollen you won't be able to walk."

Her mouth opened in shock. "Are you seriously telling me that before we go into my stepmother's house?"

"Why not? Didn't it make you wet?"

She blushed then. The color running up her neck and into her cheeks. "I'm not wet."

"Liar. I can smell your desire."

"You're disgusting," she muttered. "Why do you want me to be wet in my stepmother's house anyway?"

"It will add a layer of authenticity. Come on. Give me a quick kiss. I can see a blonde woman staring at us from the window. We don't want her to see us arguing now, do we?"

She leaned forward and quickly pressed her lips to mine. I wanted to grab her and kiss the hell out of her, but... I had time. Slowly. She would be mine before the weekend was out.

We got out of the car and walked towards the porch.

SHE KNOCKED on the door and while we waited, she tapped her heel on the ground. Other than that, she didn't look as nervous as she had in the car. Footsteps sounded on the other side of the door, then it swung open. A blonde woman opened the door. She had that Hollywood aging actress look. Flawless hair, plumped mouth, overly full cheeks, and not a wrinkle in sight. This must be Willow's stepmother.

"Willow! Your hair. It's beautiful," she cried. If one didn't know better, she gave the unquestionable impression of being ecstatically happy to see her stepdaughter.

"Hi, Nicole," Willow said in a voice that greatly

contrasted with her stepmother's. She allowed the woman to hug her, but stood stiffly and did not return the embrace. She turned towards me.

"Nicole, this is Rex Hunter, my boyfriend. Rex, meet my stepmother, Nicole."

I shook her hand. She had a firm grip. "It's a pleasure to meet you, Mrs. Garrett."

She laughed. "No one calls me that. It's Nicole, and it's a pleasure to meet you too. Welcome to our family." She tilted her head slightly and let her eyes wander behind me. "That's a nice car you got there."

"A weekend rent," I said casually.

"Of course. Well, come in out of the cold."

We entered the house after her and Willow slipped her hand into mine. It felt cold and small. It was strange and unfamiliar, but I felt suddenly protective of her. I squeezed her hand.

"Everyone is here except for the bride and groom," Nicole explained, as she walked deeper into the house.

Christmas decorations were still up, and there was a fire burning brightly in the living room. The people in the room stopped talking when we entered.

"Everyone, this is Rex Hunter, Willow's boyfriend," Nicole announced, her voice seemingly filled with pride.

A tall, dark-haired woman rose from one of the sofas. "How lovely to meet you. I'm Caroline, Willow's cousin." She turned her face to a man standing in a crowd. "And that's my husband, Kevin."

Kevin stepped forward and shook my hand warmly. "It's a pleasure to meet you."

Her sister, Olivia, was next. She hugged me, surprising

me with her friendliness. Willow took over, introducing me to the rest of her cousins, aunts and uncles.

The inevitable question came up during dinner once everyone had sat wherever they could in the living room.

"How did you two meet?" Caroline asked.

"Shall I tell them? Or will you?" I asked Willow.

"You," she said shyly.

"We met in the rain."

"Under umbrellas," Willow chipped in.

I smiled adoringly at her. "That's right. I was rushing home after work and Willow had gone out to get a hamburger." I deliberately changed the script so she would have to chime in again.

"Hot dog," she corrected. "I went out for a hot dog."

"How can I be expected to remember that little detail when I'd just bumped into the most beautiful woman in the world."

"Awww..." Olivia cooed mistily.

"Then what happened?" someone else asked.

"She covered me in mustard and ketchup," I said shortly, and everyone laughed.

"Carry on," Nicole urged, a small smile on her face.

I shrugged. "We went back to my place so I could change my clothes, then I took her out to dinner to replace her hot dog, and the rest, as they say, is history." I looked down at Willow and she was looking at me with a slightly dazed expression. I kissed her lightly on her soft mouth. This was turning out far better than I could have imagined. I was actually enjoying myself, pretending to be Willow's boyfriend.

Someone handed us a glass of white wine each and I raised mine up in gratitude. Willow tossed her glass back, finished her wine in one go, then grabbed another. She probably needed some Dutch courage.

Nicole came and took my arm. She led me to a corner of the room away from everyone. She looked up at me, her face full of sincerity.

"I can't tell you how happy I am to see Willow so happy and in love. Thank you."

Fuck. She was good. She was really good. If not for the warning from Willow, I would have eaten up her bullshit.

"You don't have to thank me. Willow is one in a million. I'm the lucky one."

"She's had a very rough year," she continued, lowering her voice. "I'm sure she's told you about Steven and her sister."

I turned to look at Willow and found her staring at me across the room. I blew her a kiss and her lips curled into a smile. Turning back to Nicole, I nodded. "She did, and I think she's awesome to want to attend the wedding." I locked gazes with Nicole. "What Tiffany and Steven did was wrong."

"Yes, of course, it was," she agreed immediately, "but as their mother everything is not black and white. You don't know how hard it is to be caught between your two daughters, even if one of them is clearly in the wrong, your first instinct is to try to keep the family together. Steven had chosen Tiffany, and that was that. There was nothing that could be done there. And I knew even though it was going to be painful for Willow for a while, she would survive, and knowing her kind heart she would move on and forgive Tiffany. I'm waiting for that day to come, I never imagined she would move on as quickly as she has though."

"Yes," I agreed, "she *has* a kind heart and she *has* moved on."

"Please be good to her. She deserves all the love and happiness she can get."

And there, just for a fraction of a second, I saw something. Something that didn't jive with the words coming out of her mouth. She was not pleased Willow had found me. Well, well.

"Oh, don't worry," I said. "I plan to shower her with love and happiness."

"If I may ask, what do you do for a living, Rex?"

"I run one of the top hedge funds in New York."

She was clearly impressed. "Oh! Sounds complicated."

"Not really," I said.

"Well, it's nice to know my daughter has found herself a man who can take care of her financially. I love them to bits, but all my daughters are high maintenance."

What kind of mother would say that to a man her daughter had brought home for the first time? A mother who was trying to put that man off. I bet she didn't say that to Steven when he declared his intentions towards Tiffany.

We both turned to look at Willow. Noticing us turn to look at her, she excused herself from the aunt she was talking to and came to join us.

I slipped my hand around her waist and kissed her cheek. Just talking to her stepmother for a few minutes had made me feel bad for Willow. Poor thing. She had put up with this subtle maliciousness all her life. Willow looked up at me, adoration gleaming from her eyes. It looked so real that for a few seconds, I felt disorientated.

My phone vibrated in my pocket. I fished it out and glanced at the screen. It was my PA. "Excuse me, I won't be long." I smiled at Willow then, weaved my way through her relatives and out of the house. Shutting the front door, I called my secretary back.

"There's an urgent email that you need to respond to," she said crisply.

"Thanks."

Disconnecting the call, I logged onto my email account, and for the next few minutes, was engrossed in responding to the email. The front door opened just as I hit send. I looked up, thinking it was Willow, but it was Caroline.

"Hi," she greeted with a friendly smile.

"Hi." I dipped my hands into my pockets.

"Just wanted to say welcome to Wisconsin," she said, coming to stand where I was. "Is it your first time here?"

"Thank you, and no it's not. I've come once for business." I didn't mention that it was a conference and I never left the hotel.

"Oh nice," she said. "You and Willow are really in love."

"Your cousin is very special to me."

"She is to all of us even if she doesn't believe it," Caroline said. "She was always very close to her father and when he passed on, it just broke her."

I kept my voice mild. "That must have been tough for all of you."

"It was. Then came the issue of Steven and Tiffany. It tore the family apart."

I nodded, not wanting to make a comment just yet.

"That was very difficult for all of us," she said and wrapped her hands around her waist.

I cocked my head to one side. "Why are you telling me this?"

"Because you're the one who is closest to Willow. We

want her to know that she's loved... and that we didn't take sides. We miss her and want her back in our lives."

"Have you tried telling her this yourself?"

"She doesn't pick up my calls, and when she does, she refuses to discuss it," Caroline said.

"Maybe this is your chance to talk to her face to face," I suggested. I didn't want to be drawn into that dispute especially as I knew how hurt Willow had been and was.

I was on Willow's side. Period.

14

WILLOW

"How are you feeling, dear?" Nicole asked, as soon as Rex moved away.

"I'm fine, thanks."

"Yes, of course, you're fine, but that's not what I'm asking," she insisted. "I'm talking about the wedding."

How the hell do you think I'm feeling? But I didn't say the words out loud. Instead, I grabbed a glass of wine from the tray that Olivia carried as she passed by. I was drinking too much, but honestly it was the only way I could cope with being cooped up in the same room with this many of my relatives.

I took a gulp and smiled at my stepmother. My jaw ached from all the smiling I'd done since I arrived. I hadn't reckoned on how exhausting it was pretending to be happy. No, not just happy, ecstatically happy.

"How can I feel bad when I have Rex?" I asked sweetly. "He's a million times the man that Steven is. Breaking up with Steven is the best thing that ever happened to me. I'll make a point to thank Tiffany for taking him off my hands."

A startled look came over Nicole's face. "That's not necessary."

"You don't think I should tell her?" I asked innocently. "She might be feeling guilty for stealing my man. It would be good for her to know she is actually the architect of my good fortune."

Nicole frowned. "Please, Willow. Just leave it. This is a happy occasion. We don't want to spoil it with any bitterness from the past."

"All right. As you wish, Nicole. Clean slate for everyone." I glanced around as if I'd just become aware that Rex was not in the room. "Rex must be wondering where I am," I murmured and turned away quickly.

I burst through the front door like someone desperate for oxygen. It felt like it too. I stopped short when I saw Caroline with Rex. Fear coursed through me. What had she asked him? Caroline was like the FBI when she wanted to know something.

I prayed Rex had kept his cool.

I went to him and he pulled me close. I could have kissed him for the way he was handling himself. He was the perfect boyfriend. Attentive but not overbearing. Loving but not nauseatingly so.

As much as this was an act, I had a feeling that Rex would make a wonderful partner. I caught myself before I delved deeper into that fantasy. Why was I even considering what Rex would be if he was a real boyfriend?

"Hey," I whispered softly.

He brushed his lips against mine, and I felt a surge of desire pulse through me. Maybe it was the wine, maybe it was nerves, but I wished I was back in the suite with Rex. Just us alone.

"I was just getting to know your boyfriend," Caroline said next to me. "I'll leave you two lovebirds alone now."

"Okay, see you later," I said without turning around.

When she returned inside the house, Rex took a step back to look into my eyes. "You look stressed."

"That, and tipsy," I added with a laugh. "Seriously though, thanks, Rex, you've been awesome. I can see the envy in their eyes." I could just imagine what my relatives were thinking. How had I managed to land a prize like Rex?

"You know, maybe some of them are just happy for you. At least, I know Caroline is," Rex observed.

I waved away his words. He had no idea what he was talking about.

"You don't know them like I do. They're all just happy that Tiffany is happy. They don't care for my happiness." All the gaslighting and pretending finally got to me and I bit my lower lip to stop myself from crying.

Rex was about to answer when a car pulled up in front of the house. I froze when my eyes zoomed in on the driver. Steven. Everything decelerated to slow motion. He opened the door and went around to open the front passenger door. Bastard. He had never once opened the car door for me.

My stepsister stepped out. She went on tiptoe and kissed Steven. Then he said something to her and she threw her head back and laughed. A burning sensation spread across my chest.

"Is that them?" Rex whispered in my ear.

"Yes," I whispered back.

Pain gripped me as I watched them walk up to the house, holding hands. They had no right to be so happy after what they'd done to me. They still hadn't noticed us yet, giving me a chance to study them. Her pregnancy was still not showing and she looked amazing.

I shifted my eyes to Steven and red, hot anger shot through me. No good bastard. As though he could feel my eyes on him, Steven looked up, his step faltering. Tiffany looked up and she too slowed down.

Rex moved closer so that our bodies were touching. They came up to us and for a few seconds, no one spoke. Rex was about six inches taller than Steven and Tiffany looked up at him, a slight frown on her face. I knew that look. It was the most incredible thing, but the blushing bride wanted Rex for herself!

Rex held out his hand to Tiffany and broke the silence. "Hi, I'm Rex, Willow's boyfriend. You must be her sister, Tiffany."

"Ah, so you're the new man. My sister always had amazing taste in men. It's such a pleasure to meet you," she simpered.

Rex turned to Steven and shook his hand. "And you must be the proud groom."

"Yeah, I'm the groom," he said in an almost defensive way. Perhaps he understood the underlying currents of change in his bride's body language.

Tiffany turned to me, her expression emanating empathy and kindness. "I hope you're okay with all this..."

My blood was boiling, but I raised an eyebrow, and pretended to look amused. "All this? "You mean your wedding?"

She nodded. "We never wanted to hurt you, Willow. You're my sister. You mean everything to me."

I bunched my hands into fists but kept them out of view by shoving them behind my back and smiled so wide, my lips hurt. "Relax, Tiffany. Its' all water under the bridge now. I'm happy. I'm with Rex."

Rex snaked his hand around my shoulders protectively, but his voice was light. "That would be me. Luckiest man on earth."

"Well, I'm happy that you're both happy," Tiffany said, sounding sick.

An awkward silence descended on us.

"We should go, darling," Rex said. "It's been a long day and I know you're tired."

"Did someone say something about leaving?" Nicole asked from behind.

I'd been so engrossed in my performance I'd not heard the front door opening. Nicole hugged Tiffany and Steven in greeting. I hated how easy their relationship looked. Fresh anger and resentment rose up my throat.

"Yes, we should be going," Rex said. "It's been lovely meeting all of you."

"Where are you staying?" Nicole asked.

"At the Lake Club," I said.

"The Lake Club?" Tiffany exclaimed. "Oh, brilliant. Steven has booked the deluxe suite there for me because I was worried about travelling through the snow in my wedding dress. So, if you ever get bored in your room, you'll be able to come visit me in my suite."

"Or you can come and visit us in the Presidential Suite," I said innocuously.

Her eyes bulged so much they almost fell out of her head. "Oh! You're in the Presidential Suite." She looked at Rex, then at me, and this time her gaze slid to the Chanel purse I was carrying. Clearly, she must have thought it was fake until this new announcement alerted her to the fact that Rex was wealthy enough to afford the Presidential suite.

She flashed a big smile, but there was a strange expression in her eyes. “Yes, I will definitely come and visit you there. I’ve always wanted to see the inside of it.”

I seemed as if I’d thoughtlessly opened a door I did not want opened. I wished I’d never wisecracked about her coming to see us in our suite.

“Right, we should be going,” Rex said firmly.

“Drive safely. These roads are dangerous when the night draws in,” Nicole advised.

“I will,” Rex responded, turning me away.

“Bye,” I called over my shoulder.

“See you guys tomorrow,” Tiffany sang brightly.

I slipped into the car and fastened my seatbelt.

“You okay?” Rex asked.

“Yup, but I’m really, really not looking forward to the hen party tomorrow.”

“I know how you feel. One of your cousins invited me to the stag night. He said it would be low key and in one of the local cocktail bars,” Rex said.

“Low-key!! Steven doesn’t know what the word means,” I spat, hating the bitterness that had crept into my voice. There were too many horrible emotions sloshing around in my body. I probably drank too much too. I needed food and I needed it soon.

“Can we please go straight to dinner?” I asked.

“Sure, why not.”

15

WILLOW

https://www.youtube.com/watch?v=Bx51eegLTY8

The hostess sat us at a cozy table for two, and a waiter brought us the food and drinks menu. Rex ordered a bottle of wine. In my head thoughts of Steven and Tiffany swirled incessantly. I hated them. Hated how they had betrayed me.

"Let's talk about something other than Tiffany and Steven," I decided.

"Be happy to. Tell me about your dad," he invited.

I smiled and felt every part of me relax. "He was a wonderful human being. So kind and humble. You would have liked him and he would have liked you too."

The waiter brought the wine. As he poured it into our glasses, my mind became awash with memories of my father. Even if Rex and I were just friends, or friends with benefits, my father would have loved him.

"I know for sure my father would have loved you," I said in a faraway voice.

An odd expression crossed his face, and his voice was sincere when he said, "I would have loved to have met him."

I think I must have been extremely nervous and stressed because I drank and talked nonstop throughout dinner. When we stood to go up to our suite, I had to loop my arm around Rex's waist to keep my balance.

When we got through the door of our suite, Rex took a step back.

"Goodnight, he said distantly.

"Goodnight," I whispered and moved away from him.

When I reached my room, I closed the door and leaned against it. Someone had come in, switched on the bed lamps, turned down the bed, and left chocolates on the pillow. I sat on the bed and ate the chocolates. They were good, but I must have been in such an emotional mess my stomach churned.

I decided to take a bath.

I ran the water in the round marble bath, poured in half the bottle of bath salts, and got in, but I couldn't relax. Something felt wrong and incomplete.

Getting out of the bath I padded over to the long mirror. There, I stood staring at myself, soapsuds dripping from my naked body onto the white marble floor.

I touched my breast. It had been so long since I was with a man. My eyes shone with some sort of unholy light, and between my legs my clit hung, hot and heavy. I stood there for what seemed like forever. Until my skin was covered with goosebumps.

Eventually, I moved away and rubbed my body briskly with a towel, bringing the warmth back to it. Almost in a trance, I dressed in my semi-transparent nightie, then brushed my hair and fluffed it out.

My bare feet were silent on the thick carpet as I walked out of my room and over to Rex's. I didn't knock on his door. I simply turned the brass handle and opened it. The lights were off, but he wasn't in bed. He was standing in front of the window looking out.

He didn't seem startled that I'd come into his room. Instead, he turned around slowly and stared at me. For a few seconds we gazed at each other, then I walked towards him and stood next to him. Outside, snow was falling again. We watched it fall in the blue light in silence. It looked beautiful, like the pages of a fairytale book.

"Why aren't you in bed?" I asked, staring at the fantastical beauty outside the window.

"I was doing what I never do."

I turned to look at him. "What's that?"

"Live in the moment. I'm always so busy I never take the time to appreciate the beauty and richness of my life."

"Abundance," I whispered, "works both ways. Why should you be stuck in this smaller room? You should have the great view of the lake I have too. We should share the main bedroom. The bed is certainly big enough for both of us."

"Okay," he murmured, and walked towards his bedside cabinet. He picked something up that was on it and came towards me.

"What's that?" I asked.

He opened his palm and I saw a box of condoms. My gaze moved up to his eyes, but it was impossible to tell what lay there.

"I like to be prepared… just in case," he said. In the pale light I saw his teeth glint when he grinned wolfishly.

"Did the big bad wolf really eat Red Riding Hood?" I whispered.

"Only one way to find out."

I put my hand out and he enveloped it inside his large warm hand.

"Come on then," I said, and led the way to the main bedroom.

In the semi-darkness of his room, I couldn't see his eyes, but I could now. In the yellow glow of the bed lamps, he stared back at me, his blue eyes were so full of hunger that his pupils were almost inky black.

He was so beautiful it was freaking me out. I could feel my blood throbbing in my ears. That's how much I wanted him.

"Tiffany wants to have sex with you," I blurted out.

"And you? Do you want to have sex with me?" he asked, his body so close to mine I could feel the heat emanating from him.

The sound of our breathing filled the room.

"I do, but won't it make things awkward between us?"

"Awkward? Not at all. I wanted to fuck you from the first moment I saw you."

"Really?" My nipples hardened and pushed against the thin material of my nightie.

"Yes, really."

"Anyway, I suppose it'll just be a weekend fling." Why the hell did I sound so breathless? Like the sort of woman who said one thing but meant something else?

"Have you ever had a weekend fling before, Willow?"

"No."

His fingers reached out and brushed my nipples, and fire whipped through my body. All from a wisp of a touch. I let out a soft sigh. Who was I kidding? All along I had known I wanted him and would probably end up in bed with him.

Wordlessly, I started to unbutton his shirt, but I didn't get very far. Rex cupped my face with his large hands, and one second later, his mouth was on mine. His tongue found mine and they entwined in hot heat.

God, he tasted good. So good, shivers went down my spine.

He drew my tongue into his warm mouth and sucked it hard as his hands moved down to cup my ass, and press me into his erection... and what an erection it was. So hard and huge. Just thinking of that massive shaft filling me up turned my body into liquid.

I felt light-headed with desire.

My hands needed to touch his skin. I fumbled again with the buttons of his shirt, but Rex ripped his mouth away and pulled his shirt over his head, leaving his muscled chest gloriously bare. Then he reached for the front of my nightie, tore it in two, and tossed it to the floor.

Rex's eyes raked over my breasts. The hunger was real.

I could feel my breasts become swollen with need, and the ache between my legs intensified. It was a long time since a man had looked at me like that. He lifted his hands to my breasts, gently rubbing his thumbs over my nipples. A moan left my mouth, as I arched my back, offering myself to him. It had been so long since I'd been with a man. I had a feeling Rex was going to spoil all other men for me.

He reached out and cupped both my breasts in his hands. "Fuck, you're even more beautiful than I imagined," he growled.

He swooped down and flicked his tongue over one sensitive nipple then the other one. He sucked gently first, then harder. I bit my lower lip to try and contain the cry of pleasure rising inside me.

"Yes," I whispered, as I caressed his shoulders, marveling at the rippling muscles underneath. Pleasure lines formed from my nipples to my very center.

I ached for Rex.

Having sex with him was... That thought lasted until Rex lifted his head and looked into my eyes. Immediately I lost all coherent thought as I stared up into his piercing blue eyes. Lust had made them shine like lapis lazuli.

He took my earlobe between his teeth, seductively. Suddenly, he grabbed a handful of my hair in hand and yanked it down so my neck was more available to his lips.

Slowly, deliberately, he trailed warm kisses against the skin of my throat, while his other hand moved to the heat of my sex. I was wearing a white thong. Instead of tearing it like he had my nightie, he only moved it aside and pushed a long finger into my dripping-wet pussy.

I inhaled sharply, as a cresting wave threatened to break inside me. I knew, when it broke, the pleasure would be incandescent. With this man it would be like nothing I have ever felt before.

"You ready, Red Riding Hood?" he whispered.

"Yes,"' I choked out.

He lifted me clean off the floor and carried me to the bed, where he laid me on the clean white linen and looked down at me. There was nothing between the big bad wolf and me except a little bit of lace.

I let my legs fall apart and his eyes flew to my open sex.

Now there was only a tiny string between the folds. That was all that kept us separate.

"Have you dreamed of this, Willow?"

"Well, I—" I began, but my words were cut off by a gasp when he plunged his finger into me again.

"A yes or no answer will suffice," he said. When he played with the soft petals of my sex, I quivered with raw need.

"Yes," I sighed. "Yes."

16

REX

https://www.youtube.com/watch?v=r3Pr1_v7hsw

Her sex was wet and spread open before me, and the tantalizing sweet scent of her arousal that I'd detected in the car earlier in the day, rose in waves from her warm pussy and called to me. She wriggled her hips as if inviting me.

I stared down at her, enthralled.

A voice in my head had been giving off a stream of warnings all day, but the voice was wrong. This was just a fling. A weekend fling in a quaint, old hotel in the middle of nowhere. Where no one knew me and I knew no one.

And why not?

I'd never been so crazy for a woman's body before. I wanted her more than I had ever wanted anyone or anything else. I got on my knees and pulled her hips up by a pointless scrap of material between us. I slipped my hands under the cheeks of her ass before I tore the lace away. Now, she was a bowl full of scent and pleasure waiting for me. There was thirst inside me, a thirst that could no longer be denied.

I dipped my tongue into her and felt a rush of intoxication.

Her taste was sweet and bright, succulent as melon dipped in honey. It was pure heaven. I could become addicted to her taste. Zealously, meticulously, I kissed the pinkest places on her pussy, and held her tightly when she arched desperately under me. When her muscles contracted and flexed, my fingers pressed even more dominantly into her flesh.

When my tongue was in her, caressing the silky wetness, she moaned with pleasure. Quickly, her sighs and moans turned to urgent cries. Her taste deepened as she got closer to her climax. Her skin flushed and she began to beg for release. I took her clit in my mouth and sucked until she screamed out, her juices flooded my mouth. I growled with hunger and need as I drank her sweetness greedily.

Eventually, she became still.

I wanted to carry on drinking her nectar, but my cock was throbbing with primal need. I rose up and saw that she was trembling, but her eyes were calm and welcoming.

"Let the wolf come out to play, Rex," she whispered.

Heat and lust throttled through my cock and raced all the way to my brain at her words. She appeared fragile and naïve, but she understood. She understood the intensity of my lust meant I couldn't be gentle. What I felt was aggressive and primitive, even furious. Until now, I'd held it back, kept it under control, resisted every pang of lust. And now it threatened to consume me.

There was no trepidation in her eyes. In fact, she welcomed it. She wanted it.

I vaulted off the bed, and in a flash, I had undressed and sheathed myself. Swiftly I went to her body and flipped it over. She gasped with surprise, but lay quietly on her stomach, her cheek resting on the bed.

Roughly, I lifted her hips so her entire pussy was exposed to me. Her pussy was swollen and slick between the cheeks of her ass.

I pushed a pillow under her hips and immediately plunged my cock into her wet slit. The motion was swift and savage. So brutal her mouth opened in shock, perhaps in pain. Nine inches was a lot for a woman to take in one thrust. Her hands gripped the sheets, but she didn't stop me. Instead, she pushed her hips wantonly into me.

Begging me to plunder her more.

For an instant, I closed my eyes, and teeth gritted, kept that last shred of control I had. Then I let go of the reined-in ferocity. My thrusts were ruthless, punishing. I fucked her like a toy. Her breathless cries rang in my ears, but I was a dark demon, possessed with wild lust for a blonde angel. I swallowed her cries, slaked my thirst, and carried on relentlessly, savagely, slamming deep into her tight, wet heat. Again, and again.

Our sweat mingled.

Suddenly, her back arched and she came, screaming my name.

My cock jerked at the sight of her white body, gleaming with sweat, and contorted with pleasure. Just like that I reached the pinnacle.

Deep inside Willow, I touched heaven and came long and hard.

Peeling off the condom, I fell forward, with half my body covering hers, my face buried in her softly fragrant hair. I was utterly spent.

When I tried to move, she spoke. "Don't."

We lay there for a time, both of us flushed. Our bodies dewy with passion and exertion. I stroked her fair hair to comfort her.

"I was too rough. Did I hurt you?" I asked.

"No. It was perfect."

17

WILLOW

My sex was swollen and sore because he'd not allowed time for my walls to stretch and accommodate his massive cock.

For one second, when he first entered me, I thought he'd split me in two. I'd never had a man with such a huge cock before. That first plunge had brought sharp pain, but because I never cried stop, because I let him do whatever he wanted to me... in the end, the ecstasy was indescribable.

For the first time in my life, I experienced multiple orgasms. I was sure Rex had ruined me forever for other men.

How would it feel to really belong to him?

Stop.

What the hell was I thinking? The way Rex had just fucked me told me everything I needed to know about how he felt about me. To him I was just a sex object. Someone he wanted to fuck for one weekend. Beyond that, he had no interest.

That was why he never revealed anything about himself to me.

Clearly, a man like him must have women throwing themselves at him on a daily basis. Just like I had done. The way Tiffany had looked at him would be forever imprinted in my mind. I even caught the longing glance the air hostess had given him when she thought no one was looking. In fact, I'd be surprised if there was a heterosexual woman alive on earth who would say no to him.

I know I should be wary, I should stomp on the brakes right now, but I was too far gone to stop it now. I needed him. My body needed the exquisite release that only he could offer. I didn't want to seem needy, but even now, I wanted the sweet pleasure of his cock deep inside me again.

"You're so quiet," Rex said. "What are you thinking?"

"How much I'd love to suck your cock." My voice trembled. I'd never been so forward with a man.

He lifted his body off me and, laying on his side, turned me to face him. "You do know how to make yourself unforgettable."

Wordlessly, I pushed him onto his back, wriggled down and pressed my lips to his cock. Instantly, it became hard with veins that popped and pulsed. He clawed his fingers through my hair.

I sucked the top of his cock, tasted our mingled juices, and decided to lick it all off. Diligently my tongue worked over the bobbing shaft, his inner thighs, and his heavy balls. I took one ball in my mouth and sucked it.

He let out a low growl, so low it sounded like it came from his belly. "Now take it all."

Well, Rex was in for a treat. I knew I could take him really deep. I took it all, every last inch, right down my throat. I heard him hiss with pleasure and surprise. My heart was thumping and I could feel my own pussy start to quiver.

I gagged on him, and tears streamed from my eyes, but I didn't stop. I carried on worshipping him. Up and down, up and down that gorgeous shaft.

When I felt his balls getting tight against my chin, I eased up so I could make him last a little longer. I loved sucking him, giving him pleasure, hearing the sounds he made. I sucked and licked him until my jaw ached.

Finally, I understood that I had kept it going as long as I could, he was bursting to come, so I began to move in a way to encourage him to fuck my mouth. He responded instantly, beautifully. The animal-like growl that rose from deep in his chest made goosebumps scatter across my chest and arms.

Grabbing my head, he spurted hot cream deep into my throat. When he was done, I greedily licked his cock clean.

"Fuck, Willow. You're something else," he whispered, as he began to finger fuck me. He added two more fingers and pounded me with them until I flew with the moon and the stars.

We fell asleep then.

18

REX

She was not next to me when I woke up. A little note was on the pillow.

If you wake up before I get back, your basket of choc muffins has arrived. Gone downstairs to get them.

With a smile I got out of bed and headed for the toilet. I was at the sink when the doorbell rang. It must be her, but I'd forgotten to put up the 'do not disturb' sign and it could be the cleaning staff, so I slipped on my pants and went to answer the door.

To my surprise, Tiffany stood outside. She was made up and dressed to the nines. Her eyes slid over my bare chest and stomach.

"Good morning," she greeted brightly.

"Good morning," I echoed quietly.

"Can I come in?"

"Er... Willow is not in."

Her eyebrows flew upwards. "Where is she?"

"I think she went to get muffins. Somewhere downstairs, but I'm not sure where."

"Can I come in and wait for her?"

I opened the wider. "Of course. Have a seat. I'll go put on a shirt."

"Don't bother on my account. Please, sit and talk with me for a minute. I'd like to get to know Willow's boyfriend."

Yeah, the way you got to know her last boyfriend. I sat opposite her and looked at her silently. If I gave her enough time, she would bury herself.

"You know, I'm so happy Willow found you. Finally, after *all* those men she's been through, you're the first good man she's had." She gave a little self-conscious laugh. "I mean, not counting Steven, of course."

The way she had emphasized the word 'all'. What a little monster! She was trying to make out Willow was some kind of nymphomaniac or slut who had slept with hundreds if not thousands of men.

She stared at me, probably wondering if she had fucked with my head yet. I experienced something I never thought I'd feel, I felt a shred of pity for Steven. He had no idea what a psycho he was marrying. I decided to do him a favor. He was not my favorite person, but even he didn't deserve this bitch.

I leaned forward. "Ah! So that's why..."

"That's why what?" she asked curiously.

"That's why Willow is so damn good in bed. Hell, she gives the best blow jobs I've ever had. She gets on her knees and she goes at it like a little fiend for ages. Steven must be missing it." I put on an expression of empathy. "She has set the standard so high it must be hard for you to keep up, let alone better her."

For a second, she was too stunned to speak. "Actually," she said coldly, "Steven said their sex life was pretty boring."

I nodded. "I suppose he would say that. What else is he going to say? We men do that. Especially, if the new woman is not as good as the previous one."

She turned purple with rage and fury. "Not every man wants a slut."

The door opened and Willow walked in holding a basket of muffins. She stopped dead in her tracks.

"What are you doing here?" Willow asked.

"Darling," I said, "Tiffany came to pay you a visit."

I watched Tiffany get herself back under control, then smile. "I wanted a tour of the suite."

"Well, you can't do it now. We've been fucking all night and the bedroom reeks of the smell of sex," Willow snapped.

To stop myself from breaking out in laughter I stood up and walked up to Willow. Taking a muffin from the basket, I bit into it. "Delicious."

Tiffany jumped to her feet. "Oh my. Is that the time? I have an appointment at the beauty salon. Bye, Rex. See you at the hen party, Willow."

"Bye, Tiffany," I called to her departing back.

Willow said nothing. She turned to me as soon as the door closed. "What did she say to you?"

I shrugged. "Nothing. She got here a few seconds before you came back. These muffins are really good."

She took a deep, steadying breath and looked at me suspiciously. "She never came on to you?"

"No," I denied immediately, and her shoulders relaxed a little.

"She's getting married tomorrow to Steven. It's not me she wants, Willow."

She shook her head exasperatedly. "God, you men are all so blind to her machinations. I know exactly what she wants. And what Tiffany wants, Tiffany gets. One way or another."

She put the basket on the coffee table and walked away. I finished the muffin first. No point wasting good food.

Then I went to look for her.

19

WILLOW

https://www.youtube.com/watch?v=Q1fGOG3XXIQ

I was so angry my hand itched to slap her!

I stood in front of the bathroom mirror and stared at my white face. Just from the way Rex answered me, I knew he was lying. She had definitely told him something uncomplimentary about me.

I knew exactly what she was up to. It was the blue blouse all over again. Anything I had she wanted it, and if she couldn't then she was going to destroy it so neither of us could have it.

How dare she?

I picked up my hairbrush and began to furiously brush my hair. I had made a date with Emma to have a quick coffee together, and now I felt too irritated and frustrated to go and pretend everything was rainbows and light.

The door opened and Rex stood at the doorway. I was

actually angry with him as well. Why did men have to be so stupid and believe all her bullshit? I guess because they all thought with their cocks and not their brains. They all fell for her fake 'I'm so small and delicate' act and her big fake breasts.

"Why didn't you put on your shirt?" I asked rudely.

His eyes narrowed dangerously to slits as he walked in and stood behind me. I was mesmerized by how his eyes glittered between his dark lashes.

"Because I have unfinished business here," he said close to my ear. Then his hands closed around me. He unzipped my jeans and unceremoniously yanked them down my thighs. Cool air hit my ass, but it was not cold for long. His warm hand grabbed the flesh and kneaded it. Without warning he ripped my little panties off and tossed them behind him. He swiped his fingers along my dripping slit, then slipped two fingers inside. I inhaled sharply.

"Still sore?" he asked.

"Yes, but don't let that stop you."

All this time his eyes never left mine in the mirror.

I heard the rustle of a packet being torn before he kicked my legs apart and lifted my hips so I was balanced on the tips of my toes. Bracing myself with my hands on the vanity unit, I spread my legs as wide as I could, then tilted my ass out and waited. He spread my ass cheeks with his hands and pushed deep into my pussy. All the way in.

I cried out with shock.

Perhaps I would never get used to how massive his cock was. He slowed for a second and sucked the side of my neck. I leaned back into him. God, I wanted him so much. I craved any touch he could give me. I yearned to have him inside me, to be stretched and filled like this, for as long as possible.

He lifted his head and gazed at me in the mirror. "Don't let her get to you, Willow. You're worth a hundred of her."

"I am?" I whispered hoarsely.

"Damn right," he snarled and almost immediately he started pounding into me. Pounding and pounding. Without stopping.

"My God," I cried, as I struggled to keep standing.

It hurt, and at the same time the pleasure that was ripping through me was so intense, my legs were shaking. I clawed at the edge of the vanity to find some balance, but I was almost like a puppet without a will. It wasn't long before I couldn't stand anymore. My legs gave way and I started to slump to the ground. Instead of stopping he kept on thrusting as he followed me to the floor.

I was on my hands and knees, my legs tangled in my jeans, while he held my hips and fucked me even more savagely. Slamming again and again into me.

I take it. And I take it.

Until I could no longer bear it and the pleasure hit me so hard it blinded me. My orgasm went on and on. I cried out, maybe I screamed, I wasn't fully conscious of what I was doing. And all the while he kept on fucking me, never slowing down until his orgasm finally took hold of him. He roared as his body slammed into me one final time. He went so deep I felt my body shudder. My eyes rolled back and I fell over the edge all over again.

It was indescribably beautiful.

I finally understood what they meant when they called an orgasm the 'little death'. When he pulled out, I crawled away from him, my jeans still tangled around my ankles, and leaned against the cold marble wall. I was reeling from the shock of how powerful and explosive the experience had been. I'd never known sex could ever be like that. Nothing I'd watched or read ever hinted of this.

I stared at him.

"She's not better than you and don't you fucking forget it," he said from the floor.

He stood, and as I stared speechlessly up at him, he casually peeled off the condom and dropped it into the toilet. Pulling up his low swung jeans, he zipped and buttoned them. "You might want to think of getting dressed. Solomon should be bringing breakfast any moment now."

Then he was gone, his bare feet silent on the white marble floor.

20

WILLOW

It took a couple of minutes before I could even stand, and when I did my legs felt like jelly. I had to grip the vanity for support. I looked at myself in the mirror and was amazed by my reflection. My face was red, my hair was a mess, and my eyes were wild. There were bruises on my hips from last night, and a love bite on my neck.

I fingered the darkening skin. Was it some sort of branding, a statement of possession? But for whose benefit? Tiffany? What had she said to him?

As I was splashing cold water onto my face and neck, I heard the doorbell. The sound of men's voices floated over together with the fragrant smell of freshly brewed coffee. I dried my face, brushed my hair, slicked on a layer of lip gloss and went out.

White sunlight was pouring in through the tall windows.

Rex was scrolling through his phone and Solomon was laying the table with what appeared to be a veritable feast.

Bread rolls, jam, honey, croissants, toast, scrambled eggs, bacon, sausages, cereal, a selection of fruit, a silver bowl filled with caviar.

"Good morning, Madam," he greeted.

"Good morning, Solomon," I replied awkwardly, my eyes sliding over to Rex.

Rex looked up at me and smiled. "Hungry?"

"Starving," I replied.

"Good."

"Shall I stay and serve, Sir?" Solomon asked.

"No, we'll be fine, thanks."

Solomon nodded. "Very good, Sir. Do ring if you need anything else."

"Thank you, Solomon," Rex said, and I echoed his words.

Solomon withdrew, and I moved closer to the table. "Would you like some orange juice?" I asked.

"No, just coffee. Black. No sugar."

He came and sat down at the table, and I sat opposite him.

"That's a lot of food for two people," I commented as I poured a cup of coffee and put it in front of him.

"I wasn't sure what you wanted."

"Will the company pay for all this?" I asked softly.

He nodded.

"Even the caviar?"

"Even the caviar," he agreed, amusement creeping into his voice.

I met his eyes head on. "You must be very valuable to the company then."

"I am," he stated simply. There was no arrogance in his expression, it was a statement of fact.

I nodded, then confessed, "I've never had caviar."

He grinned. "Ah, a caviar virgin..."

I shrugged and smiled at him. "What can I say, I'm a bit of a hillbilly."

"You are definitely not that," he said, as he used the little silver spoon next to the bowl to scoop some caviar. He set the shiny black pearls on a small round pancake and I had to admit it looked so pretty. Holding the morsel, he reached his hand across the table towards my mouth. I opened my lips and he slipped the food in.

I began to chew and... ugh... it was slimy and disgusting. My first instinct was to spit it out, but I didn't want to make a spectacle of myself so I swallowed it quickly and took a big gulp of orange juice.

"You didn't like it?" he asked surprised.

"Sorry... but it's horrible."

He started to laugh. "You are priceless, Willow."

I stared at him. "Why?"

"Because every woman I've ever been with always either genuinely loved it or pretended to. No woman I've ever been with has called it horrible."

I laughed too. "I'm a hillbilly."

"No... you're honest," he corrected.

Suddenly, I felt shame. I was not honest. I was a fraud. "Honest?" I whispered. "Look at the elaborate lie I've weaved. I'm paying you to be my boyfriend, Rex."

"Want me to be honest with you?"

"Of course."

"I actually admire you. You made a plan to save your dignity while suffering betrayal and heartbreak, and you went out and executed it perfectly. Now, stop being hard on yourself and dig into those eggs before they get cold."

I gave him a grateful smile and reached for the eggs. "The thing I don't understand is; I don't care for Steven one bit, and I wouldn't want him if he was served to me on a gold platter. But I feel insanely bad about him being with Tiffany."

"News flash, you're human, Willow. Human beings have egos and feelings. He has humiliated you and acted disgracefully. That shit hurts."

I cocked my head. "You know, sometimes I feel as if I don't know anything about you, and other times it feels like I've known you forever."

He laughed. "I'll go for known you forever."

"Seriously though, you keep a lot close to your chest," I said, warming up to the subject.

"It's cleaner like that. The less you know, the easier it will be for you to make my character up as you wish. I'm your fantasy man," Rex said with a charismatic smile, but a wary look had come upon his features.

I wanted to say more, but I knew I had to let it go.

It didn't matter, I told myself.

No, it did. Who was I lying to?

I wanted to know everything about Rex Hunter. I wanted to know why that wary look had come over him. I wanted to know all his secrets and if he wanted, I would tell him all of mine.

Crazy, but true.

"Okay." I drained the last of my orange juice, set the empty glass on the table and grinned at Rex. "I feel ready for anything now. Thank you."

"No problem. I'm always on your side, Willow. What's your itinerary for the day?" he asked, as he buttered a slice of toast.

"Well, the plan was to meet my friend Emma for a quick coffee before Tiffany's lunch hen party."

He bit into his toast. "That's weird. A hen party held at lunch?"

"Not weird at all, if you knew how my family rolls. Since Tiffany is pregnant, Nicole has decided it must be a non-alcoholic lunch for us all."

"I see."

"After the hen party I'll come back here, and we can go to Blackbeard's bar, and I can buy you that margarita. Afterwards, we'll attend the rehearsal and dinner party together."

"Sounds good."

"What will you do while I'm gone?" I asked.

"Work, walk around the lake, finish the muffins, work."

I smiled. "The sun is out today so the lake will be very beautiful."

"I'm really looking forward to it," he said, and strangely, I believed him. Even though he seemed to be a sophisticated man of the world, he really was looking forward to a walk around the lake.

THE CAR that Rex asked Solomon to arrange to take me to meet Emma dropped me off outside the Frozen Strawberry. Emma was already seated and waiting for me.

She jumped up and squealed with delight at the sight of me.

"Oh my God! Look at you. Wow! You look amazing. I love your top. It's so cute. Er... is that... a hickey on your neck?"

I blushed. "You look pretty good yourself." And she did.

She was wearing a red sweater which made her look vibrant and gorgeous.

"Sit down, sit down," she cried excitedly, "and tell me all about your new man. The whole town is freaking out about him. Chinese whispers and everything, but they are saying he's not only crazy-handsome, but as rich as Croesus."

I sat down slowly. Oh dear, I didn't think this through. This didn't feel good. I never wanted to lie to Emma and yet I couldn't tell her the truth.

"Look, Emma. It's very early days with him and me. Anything could happen. Look how long I was with Steven and how that turned out. So, I'm not counting my chickens until they are well and truly laid this time."

She deflated slightly at that. "Oh! All right. How is Queen Bitch doing? I bet she must be one of those intolerably awful Godzilla brides."

"Actually, she's been pretty good so far, but I'll tell you more after I attend her non-alcoholic lunch hen party."

Emma burst out laughing. "What?"

"I know. It was Nicole's idea. She reckons since Tiffany is pregnant and shouldn't drink, none of us should either."

Emma chuckled. "How will you bear it without alcohol?"

"I have no idea."

"Shall I go get my dad's whisky flask? You can keep it in your purse."

I laughed. "Thanks, but Nicole has probably hired a doorman to check everybody's bags as they go in."

Louis came to take the orders and we ordered a pot of coffee and a plate of their lovely strawberry shortcakes.

It was nice catching up with Emma. It was a long time

since I could just relax with an old friend. The hustle and bustle of New York was exciting, but meeting a friend who knew you inside out... I missed that.

Time flew...

21

REX

I breathed deeply, and let the cold, crisp air fill my lungs. The sun had turned the lake into a glistening mirror. The bare branches were heavy with snow. It felt good to be out here. There were some birds in the sky, other than that I was alone.

I turned around when I heard a sound behind me. To my surprise, Tiffany was coming towards me. I sighed with irritation. She was the last person I wanted to see.

"Yoo Hoo," she called cheerfully, and waved vigorously.

I didn't wave back. Eventually, she came to stand next to me. "Hi, fancy running into you here."

I didn't believe her. She was just not the walking type. She must have seen me come out here and followed. I turned to look at her. She was wearing a white coat with a fur trimmed hood which suited her. She had the kind of narrow nose only a plastic surgeon would dream up, and her mouth was too swollen, but her eyes were large and could have been pretty if they didn't have so much cunning in them.

"Your hen party should start soon," I reminded pointedly.

"I'm the star. I can be late," she dismissed lightly.

I turned away from her and carried on looking at the lake.

"You were wrong about Steven, you know? Last night, he said I gave him the best blow job he's ever had in his life."

Ah, so that had really rankled. I hid a smile. "Good for Steven," I said lightly.

"Can I talk to you about something, Rex? I think I'm literally going out of my mind, but I can't talk to anyone in my family about it. I don't know why, but I feel as if you're the only person I could talk to right now. Please."

"Go ahead," I said without enthusiasm.

"I don't think I can marry Steven," she announced abruptly.

I turned to look at her and she was wearing an expression of sadness, but her eyes were alert and she was watching me intently.

"Why? I got the impression you were both deeply in love."

"I know Steven loves me, but I'm not sure I do."

"You really should talk to your mother about this. It's probably just bridal nerves," I suggested.

"It's not bridal nerves. I've been feeling this for the last two weeks, only I haven't had the courage to do anything about it because the wedding is so close. But now, after I've seen the way you are with Willow, it's made me think that I've made a terrible mistake. Steven is not actually right for me. He's not the man I dreamed of."

"He may not be the man you dreamed of, but he'll probably make a good father to your child," I said mildly.

"I'm not pregnant," she blurted out.

I stared at her with surprise. "What?"

She bit her lip. "Well, it started out as a mistake. You know, I thought I was pregnant so I took a test and it must have been a false positive, but I didn't know better, so I told Steven I was. He was so happy he proposed to me. By the time I took the second test that showed a negative result, everyone was so happy and excited, I didn't have the heart to tell them. I mean, Steven actually went out and bought some baby sleepers."

"What will you do in eight months when Steven will be expecting to put his child into those sleepers?"

"Oh, I was never intending to carry it on until then. My plan was to have a miscarriage in a couple of weeks. I was thinking after the honeymoon, but now it's starting to look like that might not even happen."

I looked at her curiously. I was looking at one of the most selfish, manipulative women I'd ever met, and I had met a few in my line of work. It was almost certain she was never pregnant, she simply made it up to coerce Steven into proposing.

She cast her eyes down, as if she was feeling guilt. "Oh, Rex. I know you must think I'm a terrible person, but I'm just so confused. I honestly feel like doing what Willow did; running away to the city, starting again, and maybe finding someone like you."

She looked up again and gazed at me with a pleading look in her eyes.

"If I do go to the city, will you give me your number so I know I will be safe. So, I know I'll have someone to turn to if things get bad. Not financially or anything, but just so I have a strong shoulder to lean on in case I get into any sort of trouble."

I could hardly believe Steven could be so stupid as to fall for this kind of outright manipulation. She was so obvious, it was laughable. I played along.

"The best thing you can do if you get in trouble is to call Willow, and if necessary, she'll call me and I'll see what I can do to help."

She wrung her hands together. "I don't know how much Willow has told you about our relationship, but she kinda hates me. When my mom married her dad and we moved into his home, Willow took an instant dislike to me, and no matter what I did, she hated my guts. But I hero worshipped her. Once, I borrowed her blue blouse because I loved it so much. She was so angry she ripped it to shreds rather than let me have it. I mean, you saw how she was with me this morning when I came to your suite."

"I'm sorry, Tiffany, but I can't get between you and Willow. You'll have to sort your differences out without me."

There was a flash of fury in her eyes, but she nodded, and said meekly, "I understand, but please think about what I said, Rex. You have no idea how much you would be helping me."

"Goodbye, Tiffany. Enjoy your party."

"Thanks a lot for listening, Rex. It's really helped to unravel things in my head. Umm... please don't tell anyone, not even Willow, what I told you. I'll tell everyone in my own time and in my own way."

Then she turned away and started walking back towards the hotel.

22

WILLOW

My stomach churned with anxiety as my feet got closer and closer to the Green Bison restaurant. In just twenty-four hours I'd gotten used to having Rex with me when I had to face my family. He was my shield, making me feel safe and protected from my own family.

Now, I was going to have to face them alone.

My feet faltered, but I took a deep breath and gave myself a firm pep talk. No, I was not going to be a little coward. None of what had happened was my fault. I wasn't the betrayer or the boyfriend stealer.

I smiled as I recalled the look of surprised admiration on everyone's face when they met Rex. I threw my shoulders back. I had no reason to be anxious when everyone was under the impression I'd landed myself the ultimate man.

All I had to remind myself over and over again was: Steven and Tiffany had done me a favor when they slept with each other behind my back. By the time I reached the doors of the restaurant I was grinning and raring to go.

They had booked the whole restaurant for the party and it was decorated with strings of tiny lights and gorgeous center flowers on each table. I started to frown when I noticed large, photographer-quality photos of Steven and Tiffany hanging on all the walls. Great, they were going to be in my face the whole freaking time.

Caroline was the first to notice me. She smiled at me and started walking towards me.

"Hi and welcome," she said, her eyes sliding to the love bite on my neck. "We weren't sure whether you'd come."

My own smile faltered a little and immediately I went on the defensive. "Why would I not come? I haven't wronged anybody."

"No, you haven't. By the way, I love your top," she complimented quickly.

Tiffany stood up from where she was sitting and came over.

"Hi," she said. Her eyes also instantly clocked the love bite on my neck, but there was something else in her eyes. Anxiety about tomorrow? Or was it guilt?

"Hi," I said, smiling as if I was ecstatic to be there.

"I was just telling Willow how lovely her top was," Caroline said.

Tiffany let her gaze rove over my clothes. A frown appeared on her brow. "Is that top from Gucci's new season?"

I shrugged carelessly. "I wouldn't know. I'm not into fashion. A personal shopper found it for me."

Tiffany's eyes widened with surprise and envy. "You have a personal shopper?"

"Actually, she's a friend of Rex's. She has very good taste," I said casually.

Tiffany and Caroline looked at each other. I bet they wished they hadn't invited me. Well, by the time their pathetic, alcohol-free party was over, I planned to leave them in no doubt I was more than okay. I moved away, determined to have fun.

"Hey you, I made some non-alcoholic cocktails. Try one," Olivia said loudly, shoving a tray in front of me.

I glanced at the lurid cocktails without interest.

She leaned close and whispered, "Try the green ones. They are lethal. I made them green because Tiffany hates green."

I grabbed a drink from the tray and tossed it back, placed the empty glass, and took another one.

"Let the party begin," I said, and Olivia winked at me.

She wasn't exaggerating. The cocktails were lethally strong. I could feel their warmth spreading from my stomach up to my chest, then run like fire through my veins. Good. It was exactly what I needed.

I was seated on the table with the bride, Olivia, two of my cousins, and Tiffany's friend. We said hello, but I didn't miss the look they all exchanged. Well, I was going to show them that I was absolutely okay with Tiffany marrying Steven. Absolutely, completely, and totally.

Lunch was served, and I believe it was good, because everyone else said so, but I barely ate, moving it around my plate until it was cleared away.

"It was nice to meet Rex," my cousin Ashley said. "He's a catch alright."

I swelled with pride. "Rex is awesome. He can't do enough for me," I said, loud enough for my voice to reach Tiffany.

Everyone smiled including Tiffany, even though her

smile was more than a little forced. I wonder whether she still thought Steven was a catch when she compared him to Rex.

I seriously doubted it.

After lunch, it was time to play a game. I stifled a yawn. The idea of playing a game didn't sound like fun, until Caroline explained the rules. We were playing 'I solemnly swear I've been up to no good.' It involved writing down on a piece of paper something you had done that was either raunchy or crazy.

The alcohol sang in my veins and I shivered with excitement. My phone vibrated in my pocket. It was a message from Rex.

I'm hard for you.

My face heated up even more. It felt as though everyone on the table could read the message. I typed out a reply.

You just made me wet.

"Are you having a good time?" Caroline asked.

I hit send and put my phone away. "Yes, it's a nice party. You've done a good job." I wanted to, but didn't add, hosting a cheat and a boyfriend stealer.

"Yeah, with no help from you," she murmured.

I stared at her in shocked amazement. "What's that supposed to mean?"

"It means that you're never here for our family," Caroline scolded in a hushed voice. "You have always been busy living your fabulous life with no thought to the family you left behind in Wisconsin."

Red, hot anger coursed through me.

Unfortunately, Tiffany chose that moment to appear next to us. It set me off. I pointed a finger at her. "She fucked my boyfriend. How the hell am I supposed to help plan her wedding?"

A tense silence followed my words.

"I thought you had no problem with it," Tiffany said, a sly smile on her face.

I resisted the urge to hiss. This was not the behavior of a happy, satisfied woman. Holding myself tightly in check, I smiled, and I could tell the sudden change confused them.

"I have no problem whatsoever with you marrying Steven. Once a cheat, always a cheat." I spotted a tray with fresh cocktails, grabbed a green one, and took a big sip. Now in my element, I continued. "I found the man of my dreams and I'm happy." I sounded so genuine I almost had myself fooled.

"Good, in that case, we can continue with the party," Caroline said.

Caroline and Olivia passed out small pieces of papers and pens to everyone. You were supposed to write your confession and the bride would read them aloud and guess who had written it.

I wrote mine and when the basket came around, I tossed my folded paper in. When all the papers were collected, Tiffany stood up and picked the first paper. Dramatically, she looked at all of us before slowly opening the first paper. My heart pounded with anticipation. Would mine be first?

"I solemnly swear I've been up to no good," she read. "I'm single and last night, I had the greatest sex of my life."

We all burst out laughing.

I looked around at the twenty or so women and couldn't

imagine who would have written it. It turned out to be Tiffany's friend who good-naturedly admitted to having written the note.

The tension dissipated and even I found myself giggling as Tiffany read out the outrageous notes. For a few seconds, I began to regret the note I'd written, then I reminded myself what Tiffany had done. She was not the innocent person she was portraying herself to be.

She picked up a note, straightened it, cleared her throat, and read.

"I confess that last night, I had a very raunchy night with my boyfriend whom I did not steal from anyone I know."

I raised my chin as everyone looked at me. Nonchalantly, I picked up my drink and took a sip.

"I'm guessing this is from you, Willow," Tiffany said, her teeth gritted.

"How did you guess?" I asked in a friendly tone.

Her chin wobbled and shame came over me. I knew I'd gone a tad bit too far, but once I'd started, I couldn't stop. An image of Tiffany telling me she was fucking my boyfriend filled my mind. The guilt disappeared. I'd done the right thing. She deserved this and more.

She continued with the rest, but the fun was gone. I'd achieved my purpose, showing everyone what this was about. We were not going to pretend that it was a normal wedding. My stepsister had stolen my boyfriend.

I finished my drink and grabbed my purse. Without saying anything to anyone, I stood up. It was time to leave. I walked towards the restaurant and just as I grabbed the door handle, I heard Caroline's voice behind me.

"Did you have to do that?" she asked angrily.

I whirled around. "Do what?" I asked with feigned innocence.

"Spoil the evening for Tiffany? Don't you think she's suffered enough?"

"What? How has she suffered?" I gasped.

"Everyone knows what she did. It can't be easy being labelled as a boyfriend snatcher. But your behavior is making sure all that sympathy is going to Tiffany."

My pulse speeded up and my muscles quivered with anger and indignation. "I'm not looking for sympathy," I hissed. "I'm just having fun at my stepsister's hen party while sticking to the truth. I'm not going to pretend that this wedding is anything more than what it is."

"You've become a bitter person, Willow," Caroline said.

Her words cut deep. I didn't want to come out as bitter. The purpose of coming to the wedding had been to show everyone I was fine. I glanced at my watch in an attempt to save my reputation.

"I've got to go. Rex will be waiting for me. I promised him margaritas at the bar," I said breezily.

I turned and left. My heart was beating rapidly. Before the conversation with Caroline, I'd have concluded the lunch had been a smashing hit.

But being called bitter? That had shaken me. I needed to polish up my acting skills. I shouldn't have written that confession. It had exposed the pain in my heart over my stepsister's betrayal.

23

REX

I took one look at her face and knew the hen party hadn't gone well. She smiled softly at me. "I promised you margaritas at the bar."

"You did," I said, and stood.

She pressed her lips together. "Do you think I'm bitter, Rex?"

"No."

She frowned. "Are you sure?"

"Why, who thinks you're bitter?"

"Caroline. But to be fair to her I was a bit of a bitch today. I couldn't help myself. Every time I looked at Tiffany, the image of her sitting on the edge of my sofa as if it was dirty, and telling me she stole my boyfriend while pretending to cry fills my head, and I feel such a rage I just want to slap her smirking face so hard I break her jaw."

God, she was beautiful when she was angry. I wanted to fuck her right there at the door. "So, you're not wet for me anymore?"

"Dry as a nun's clit at the moment, I'm afraid," she surmised.

I chuckled. "Will a few margaritas help?"

She smiled. "Maybe. I know you've had to hear me go on and on about my ridiculous situation, but you do know that I'm glad my relationship with Steven ended, don't you? He wasn't right for me at all. I can see that even more clearly now. We are too different and he didn't deserve me."

No, he fucking didn't. Only a fool would drop a gem like Willow for a shallow, worthless creature like Tiffany.

"I'm glad you realize that now," I said, an uncomfortable sensation clawing my gut. It took me a few seconds to realize what it was. I thought the lady doth protest too much and I was...

Jealous!

I was in a jealous rage as if she was mine. Jealous that that asshole had ever even touched her. The intensity of the sensation made me clench my hands with black fury.

What the fuck was wrong with me?

What did it matter what they had done in the past? To start with I was not the jealous type, and I definitely wasn't in the market for a relationship with anyone. Period. Willow and I had strong chemistry, but we were ships sailing past each other, but had stopped to fuck hard, before each went on its separate journey.

We were that fucking temporary.

"You're not listening to me. What are you thinking about so seriously?" she asked.

I held her gaze. "Fucking you."

She choked. "What?"

"You heard."

"Damn, Rex. You really know how to turn a girl on," she murmured throatily.

"Back to your bed?" I suggested.

She licked her lips saucily. "No. I feel dirty, and not in a good way. Shower first, I think. Wait for me here."

First, she kicked off her shoes, then as she walked, she discarded more and more clothes leaving a trail of them in her wake. Her panties, she threw in my direction, just before she disappeared through the bedroom door.

I caught the scrap of lace in my hands and brought it up to my nose. Instantly, the image of Willow's wet, pink pussy dropped into my head, 3D, and in full color.

All the blood in my body dropped to my cock, making me steel hard.

"Wait here," she said. The smart thing, of course, was to stay away from the fucking bathroom for at least a few seconds. Give the woman a chance to use the toilet in peace and wash a little before I jumped her.

I pulled out my phone. There were several messages, all related to work. Nothing that couldn't wait.

Fuck. I couldn't do it.

I couldn't fucking stay away.

The sound of the shower floated into the room and with it, the image of a naked Willow with water cascading down her hot body. That did it. I got up, dumped my clothes on the floor and went towards the bathroom.

She'd left the door open and her form was blurry though the shower wall. She slid the shower door open and I stepped into that large steamy space. Wordlessly, she poured a generous helping of shower gel into her hand. Starting from my shoulders, she rubbed it all over my body, skipping my raging cock.

"You missed a bit," I commented, when she turned me around.

Her laughter rang out and bounced off the marble surfaces. "No. I'm saving the best for last."

She rubbed the gel into my back. "Now turn around and stand under the water," she commanded.

I obeyed and watched her movements as she poured more shower gel into her hand.

She wrapped her hand around my cock and gently soaped it. A hiss escaped my mouth. It felt so fucking good to have her hands on me. If my cock grew any harder, I felt as if it was going to fucking rip apart.

Willow washed my cock and balls and let the water rinse away the lather. She shot me a mischievous look before dropping to her knees. She held my cock in both hands and looked up at me.

"It's reward time for being so patient."

"It's a good thing then that you can't read my mind," I said.

"What are you thinking?" she said.

"It's punishment time for you," I quipped.

She laughed and took my cock into her mouth, taking all of it in one go. I let out a long groan, and she pulled out and did the same again.

Fuck, I almost came.

If she kept it up, I was going to come before we did anything. Gently, I extricated myself from her mouth and pulled her to her feet.

"What?" she asked with a pout.

I wrapped my hands around her waist and pulled her close. Her lips gleamed from the water as I captured her lower one for a greedy nibble. Willow threw her hands around my neck and caressed the back of it.

She tasted of some sweet alcohol and candy. Our tongues swirled and teased while our bodies pressed against each other.

"God, I really need to fuck you," I said.

"I'd never have suspected," she quipped.

I laughed and turned off the water. Stepping out of the shower, I grabbed two towels and handed one to Willow.

We dried off and left the towels in the bathroom. Leading her to the bed, I laid her on it. I needed to kiss every inch of her. Languidly, I kissed her neck and shoulders, before dipping down to her breasts. I cupped them together and licked and kissed until she moaned and urged, "Don't stop. Please."

"No chance," I assured.

What was it about Willow that kept me coming back for more? She was beautiful, but I'd had women more beautiful than her.

There was the sex, of course. Greatest I'd ever had with any woman. No comparison. Or was it maybe, for once in my life I was playing the knight in shining armor and enjoying the ability to so effortlessly rescue her from her problems.

I dropped to my knees, spread her long, long legs open and dipped my head to her sweetness. "You smell so hot."

"Oh God, Rex," she moaned at the first contact of my tongue on her soft, sweet folds.

I found her throbbing clit, and teased it mercilessly with my tongue. Willow's movements grew more and more frenzied as she edged closer and closer to orgasm. I slipped two fingers inside and fucked her with them. Hot juices gushed out of her but it never made its way lower.

I drank them thirstily.

Her body gave a sudden jerk, then quivered like a string on a bow as she came. I rose to my feet and reached for a condom. She lay spread open, gazing at me through slitted eyes.

"I don't think I can move my legs," she said, sounding pleased at the disability.

I laughed. "Don't worry, for what comes next you won't have to move a muscle."

24

WILLOW

I was standing in front of the bathroom mirror looking at my reflection when Rex came to stand behind me. He stared at my reflection silently, passion and craving burned in his eyes.

I was wearing charcoal eyeshadow, bright red lipstick, and the green dress with a high slit up one thigh.

Silently, he fitted the emerald necklace Nina and I had picked at the jewelry store around my neck, and snapped the clasp. Then he attached the matching bracelet on my wrist. Gazing at me in the mirror, he moved the necklace aside and, lowering his head, kissed me on the very spot he'd left his mark.

"You look stunning," he murmured into the bruise. "If I wasn't already on a dirty weekend with you, I'd have to take you on one."

A tingle went through me. "More of that talk and I don't think my legs will hold me up."

Rex looked up and laughed, the corners of his eyes crinkling. My breath hitched as I stared at him. He was so beautiful. What would it feel like to wake up to his insanely handsome face every morning, knowing that it was forever?

My wayward thoughts were treading on dangerous ground. Thinking about Rex like that would only lead to heartbreak. I believed some people came into our lives for a season and then left.

Rex was one of those people.

The universe had conspired for us to meet so that he could help me out when I really needed it. The mistake usually came when we tried to hold on to people who were only destined to be in our lives for a short time.

"The rest of the jewelry you need for tomorrow is in the safe. The passcode is 474792."

The fact that he completely trusted me with these terribly expensive pieces made me feel oddly emotional. A soft, wistful sigh escaped my mouth.

"Okay, I'll return these tonight," I said. My voice sounded distant, and far away.

He ran both his hands over my hips and buttocks possessively. "You have a very sexy ass, and tonight, I'm going to make it mine."

I stared at him in the mirror. "I've never done that with anyone before, but yes. You can take it, if you want. It's all yours."

"A caviar and anal virgin? Willow, you're destroying me," he mocked, but there was deep hunger lurking in his eyes. Desire throbbed in the air and I could feel myself being pulled into its irresistible web. I swallowed hard.

"We should leave, else we'll be late," I mumbled.

Rex stepped back. "We're already late."

He thrust his hand forward so I could see his wristwatch.

I gasped. "What? We're already nearly half an hour late. Let's go."

"You know who is to blame for that," he mocked, as I hurried towards the door.

"I didn't hear you complaining then."

"You don't hear me complaining now," he replied dryly, catching up to me.

I felt bad about our tardiness, but I hoped everyone would be having such fun that they wouldn't notice our late entrance.

No such chance. Once again, my family had reserved the whole restaurant and when Rex and I walked in, hand in hand, the conversation didn't just taper off, it completely stopped, and everyone turned to stare at us.

"About time," my big-mouthed cousin Jody said.

I met my stepmother's eyes. I knew that look. She was pissed off. Well, I wasn't the bride. So, what if we were a few minutes late. Okay, maybe not a few minutes. Half an hour to be exact.

"Sorry we're late," I sang breezily. "But we're here now."

"Your seats are here," Caroline said, gesturing at two empty chairs at the main table where my family sat.

Reluctantly, I trailed after Rex. I'd rather have sat anywhere else but there, but with everyone watching us with a mixture of curiosity and fascination, I had no choice.

"Why couldn't you make it on time? Aren't you staying in this hotel anyway?" Nicole asked, her voice deliberately bland.

"Rex and I..." I shot him a secret look. "Well, let's just leave it at we couldn't help ourselves."

Rex nudged me under the table and I made myself shut up, but I'd achieved a reaction from my family. Nicole was outraged, Caroline looked thunderous, and some of my younger cousins were giggling. Steven was staring at his empty glass with an oddly embarrassed expression, and most importantly, the bride looked pissed off enough to walk out of her own rehearsal dinner.

Good. Let them know how awesome the evening had been for me so far.

I barely ate and instead drank two glasses of wine in quick succession. Consequently, I felt the effects immediately. I was walking on air and nobody could bring me down.

"Willow," Olivia said loud enough for everyone in the room to hear. "My best friend and I are travelling to New York on Thursday. We're flying in and taking the night bus back. She's going to do dinner with her aunt, so how about Rex, you and me meet up for dinner?"

That took me aback and for a second, panic came over me. Every eye in the room was focused on me. I thought quickly. "It would have been wonderful for us to meet," I turned to face Rex, "but you're away then, aren't you?"

"Actually, I'm not and it's a great idea," Rex said smoothly. He turned to face Olivia. "If you can get to Willow's apartment, I'll send a car to pick both of you up."

"Oooo... brilliant," Olivia crowed.

My surprised gaze flew to Rex. He looked down at me and smiled very lovingly. "We'll make a night of it."

"Okay," I said, smiling back, even though I didn't know what the hell he was playing at. Tomorrow was supposed to be our last day together.

"I feel as if I've seen you somewhere before, Rex," Steven's best man said. "Have you been to Chicago before?"

Rex shook his head. "I probably look like someone you know."

"Yeah, but have you been to Chicago?" the man insisted.

"Sure, loads of times, but I'm pretty sure we haven't met."

He frowned. "I know we haven't met, but I have seen you somewhere before. I never forget a face. What is it that you do?"

Everything was going wrong. Rex was becoming the object of their focus. I jumped to my feet, determined to take the attention away from us. I raised my wine glass and my bracelet sparkled under the chandeliers. I smiled brightly. "I know you're all very curious about Rex and me, but tonight, it's about Steven and Tiffany. So, I'd like to propose a toast."

I inhaled deeply to steel myself. "Congratulations you two," I said to a room so hushed, I could hear myself breathing. I caught the loving look Steven gave Tiffany and pain funneled into my heart at the stark reminder that he'd picked her over me, but I smiled like a proud older sister. "I wish you happiness and all the good things life has to offer." Then I leaned forward as if the next bit was only meant for Tiffany's ears.

"I hope you appreciate what an act of generosity giving you my leftovers was," I said and laughed conspiratorially.

"That's enough, Willow," Caroline said, standing up and facing me as if daring me to continue.

"It was a joke," I protested. "Seriously though, I wish you all the best." I turned to Rex. "You got the best part of me."

I sat down before Caroline could ask me to.

I didn't have to look at everyone's faces at the table to know they were fuming. As soon as I sat down, the euphoria I'd been riding on subsided, leaving me cold and more than a little shaken by my own behavior. The words I'd said repeated in my brain like a bad recording. That had been downright nasty.

Sure, Tiffany had hurt me badly, but I'd just humiliated her in front of everyone.

As things went back to normal, Greg, Steven's best man, announced that it was time for the introductions. Steven and Tiffany went first. He shot me a worried glance, probably worried that I would say something inappropriate. He had no reason to worry. I was done.

I felt spent and oddly empty.

My chest squeezed painfully when I realized that Tiffany was actually lapping it all up by looking embarrassed and scared, while Steven stroked her hair and whispered something in her ear. She'd been playing the part of the victim her whole life and all I had done with my childish performance was put myself in the position of the bad guy again and given her another opportunity to play the old default role of 'poor Tiffany'.

Nicole and my half-sister stood and started to introduce themselves. I didn't, figuring everyone knew who Rex and I were by then. The strangers at Greg's table stood up and as they introduced themselves, I realized with horror that they were giving Tiffany looks of encouragement and comfort. They knew her well, and liked her. Steven had never once suggested I meet a member of his family. He must have always known we had no future.

I was glad when the introductions were over and everyone was invited to socialize. Nicole stood up and came to my side of the table.

"Can I speak to you for a moment?" she asked, a tight smile on her face.

"Sure," I said cheerfully, and kissing Rex full on the mouth, followed her out of the restaurant to a room off the hallway. Here there was no chance of anyone overhearing our conversation.

We stood facing each other without talking.

"I'd hoped that you girls would have let bygones be bygones by now," she said quietly.

What was she trying to do? Make me feel sorry for Tiffany. She had hurt me dammit!

"Why do you pretend that everything is okay? That this is a normal marriage?" I asked angrily. I was tired of pretending. "It's not. Tiffany stole him from me," I hissed. "And you made her think that it was okay. You all did."

I hated the tears that filled my eyes. The last thing I wanted was to show weakness, but I couldn't seem to control my emotions.

"It wouldn't have made a difference what I thought of their relationship. They were still going to go ahead with it."

She made sense, but I didn't want to be sensible. I folded my arms across my chest stubbornly. I was not going to let her gaslight me into thinking I was the one being unreasonable.

"There's something else I want to say to you," she added.

"What?"

"A human being cannot be stolen. Steven made a choice to have an affair behind your back and leave you for another woman who, unfortunately happens to be your sister."

"What?" I nearly yelled, consumed by fresh anger. "You think that's helping?"

Her face hardened. "I think it's a truth you need to understand."

"I've had enough," I said. "I'd hoped you would apologize on her behalf. Instead, you're insinuating that my anger is pure churlishness."

Fuming, I whirled on my heel, and returned to the restaurant. I plastered a smile and entered, spotting Rex speaking to my Uncle Fred. He looked like he was having a good time. I made a beeline for him, but before I reached him, Steven intercepted me.

"Hey," he said.

"I can't believe you've the nerve to come and speak to me after what you did. It's only a matter of time before my sister finds out just what kind of a man you really are. Oh, and I'm using the word 'man' loosely."

"You don't let up, do you?" he said. "Listen, I just want to say I'm sorry for the way I went about it. But I'm not sorry that I'm with Tiffany. You and I were all wrong for each other and you know that."

If he thought I was going to let him off the hook he had another thing coming. "So that gave you the right to fuck my sister?"

He cringed. "Stop it, Willow. You've made the point you came to make. All you're doing now is making people feel pity for you because you obviously still have feelings for me."

"What? Are you insane?" The idea was so ridiculous, I started to laugh. Loudly. So loud, it drew other people's attention, including Tiffany.

"Is everything all right?" she said, joining us.

"Oh yes," I said, wiping tears from the sides of my eyes. "I never knew Steven could be this funny."

25

REX

"Are you still in love with him?" I asked as we walked back to our suite.

"What?" Willow exclaimed, sounding genuinely shocked at the idea.

But the past had shown me that women were born with acting ability. An image of Willow throwing her head back and laughing uproariously filled my mind. A vise clenched my insides.

"I've never seen you laugh as you did tonight with Steven." I hated the alien feelings that had come over me. The jealousy that was eating me alive and not letting me think rationally.

Willow sighed heavily. "That was a sarcastic laugh. And anyway, who wouldn't laugh, if they're caught in the mess I'm in?"

I had no reason to be proprietorial over Willow. The fact that we were going at it like rabbits day and night did not give me exclusive rights. We were supposed to be acting. At any rate, there was no reason at all for me to be having these thoughts and feelings. I didn't want to be in a relationship. Period. There was no place in my life for an all-consuming relationship.

We were close to the elevator, when she stopped and turned to me.

"Why did you tell Olivia that we can have dinner together?"

I shrugged. "I'll be in New York that day, so I thought, why not? Might be fun."

"But our agreement..."

"Don't worry, I'm not going to charge you more for one more night of acting."

She frowned and was about to say something else, but I spoke first. "Well, I guess I'll see you later."

"Why, where are you going?" she asked, her voice small and almost desperate.

"Steven's stag party." To be honest it was something I dreaded, but I needed a distraction from Willow. I needed a bit of time away from her body, to get some perspective, to stop thinking with my dick.

"Go on up. I need to make some business calls anyway. I'll see you when I get back."

She stared at me for a moment. "Okay."

I watched her get into the elevator and as the doors slid shut, I took a left and went to the hotel bar. Blackbeard's Bar was muted and quiet with only a few people occupying the tables.

I headed to a private table in a corner.

As soon as I sat down, I immediately wished Willow was seated across from me. No woman had ever captivated me as much as she had. She had worked her way into my every thought in the little time we'd known each other. It was actually pretty crazy how I saw her in every situation in my life, next to me.

The waiter pulled me from my thoughts when he came to take my order.

For a moment, I considered ordering a margarita, but it felt wrong to be drinking it without her. I ordered a bourbon on the rocks instead, and when the waiter retreated, I got busy on my phone. There were only two important items that needed my attention, the rest I forwarded to my PA.

The waiter brought my drink.

I tossed it back and set the glass back on the table, and left for what I knew was going to be a dreary experience replete with the obligatory strippers, too much booze, and grown men behaving like fools.

26

WILLOW

A strange pang of disappointment and loss came over me when I stood in the elevator and watched Rex walk away from me. It was a horrible feeling and it made me fear what would happen when the weekend was over, when he really walked away for good.

Was I falling too deeply in lust with him?

I went up to our bedroom, showered, then changed into one of his shirts. After putting away my borrowed clothes and jewelry, I slipped between the sheets with my phone.

The bed smelled of Rex, making me miss him even more. I clicked on my phone and found new messages from the dog hotel. I smiled at the pictures of Pogo having fun with the others.

Good. At least he was having a good time and not making a complete fool of himself.

The plan was to stay awake and wait for Rex, but before too long, my eyes were droopy with sleep. *I'll close my eyes just for a little while*, I told myself.

I WOKE up to find someone had gently parted my legs and was sucking on my pussy. I stretched with pure pleasure, as he pushed his tongue deep into my sex.

"Don't stop. It's nice," I whispered.

"The smell of you drives me crazy," he said, his voice muffled by my wet flesh.

I moaned as he continued to eat me until I climaxed, and yet he didn't stop his ministrations. He kept on sucking my pussy lips before taking his tongue down across my perineum to the tight opening of my ass.

"Oh," I cried with surprise when he began to lick at the opening. Boy, was I glad I showered before getting into bed.

He lapped back and forth across it, licking a little harder each time, sometimes returning to suck my clit. Eventually, he rimmed my asshole, coating it with saliva, then he pushed the tip of his tongue against the tight muscle.

It was a strange sensation to have his tongue gripped inside the tight muscles of my ass. He slipped out and continued coating my anus with saliva. A little harder, and a little deeper each time until he was tongue-fucking my ass. It was a fantastic sensation, and I heard myself cry out, "Oh fuck, yes!"

He collected the slick juices from my pussy on his finger and started to slowly push it into my ass.

I gasped.

"Tell me to stop, if it's too much," he said.

"No, carry on, but it feels so big and it's only your finger."

"Yes, you're very tight, but you can take it," he whispered as he gently finger-fucked my ass.

"Oh," I said as his entire finger finally slid deep into me.

"Do you like my finger in your ass, Willow?" he asked.

"Yes," I confessed.

"You're a bad girl, Willow."

"You're a bad man, Rex."

"Then let's be bad together," he said softly and, bending his head, sucked my clit.

With his hands around my ankles, he lifted my legs up and apart, and pulled me almost onto my shoulders. He leaned forward until his cock found my wet pussy and slipped inside. I was so soaked; his entry made a wet squelching sound. He drove into me, filling my depths with his cock.

"Yes, yes," I cried restlessly, until without real warning, a strong orgasm washed over me like a giant wave. My whole body contracted, I could feel myself squeezing and trapping his finger inside my body. He dipped his thumb into my sopping wet pussy.

"Relax, Willow, relax," he instructed, as he very gently inserted his slick thumb into my ass. It was much thicker, but it slid in without too much trouble. I could feel how slippery he had made my anal passage.

"It's time, Willow," he whispered, and moved me to the edge of the bed and into a kneeling position. "This way you won't be bouncing on the bed for your first time. Now, stick that sweet ass out for me."

I pushed my bum out. "Like this?"

"Exactly, like that," he said, and licked along the valley between my ass cheeks. He placed a tube of lube at the very place he had licked and squirted a generous amount of the cold gel inside and all around my anus. Turning around, I watched him lube his cock. It looked iron hard, the veins popping aggressively.

"Mmmm... that feels good," I murmured, as he teased my anus with his finger, slowly sliding in and out, working the lube into me.

"Now two fingers," he said, and slowly pushed in. "Does it hurt?"

"No... maybe a little. I feel stretched."

"Good," he said and began to turn his fingers inside me, stretching me further. Gripping his cock tightly, he placed the tip at my anal passage and pushed gently forward.

"You look beautiful like this, with my cock spearing your ass," he said, as his cock clipped past the first set of muscles.

"Oh God," I exclaimed breathlessly. "You're so damn big, but I want to take all of you into me. I want to be full of you. All of you. Every last inch."

He pushed further in, then squirted more lube. He must have been halfway in at least, when he started moving back and forth inside me. Every thrust went deeper.

Wantonly, I pushed my ass towards him, welcoming him.

He leaned forward and sucked my neck. I turned my head, and he forced his tongue into my mouth, so ferociously it was almost like a tongue fuck. He had held back for so long, but I could feel his excitement begin to peak now.

"Ready?" he whispered finally.

"Yes," I whispered.

"Here it comes. All of it," he said, and gripping my hips he filled me completely.

"Awww... it hurts like the blazes, but I don't want you to stop."

Using his thumbs, he opened my cheeks even more,

allowing the last inches of his hard shaft to enter me. It was beautiful to know I had taken all of it.

He bent his head and kissed me again. "Well done, Willow. It's your first time, I won't pound you too hard. Just relax." Gradually, he pulled his cock almost all the way out, then unhurriedly drove it all the way back into me.

Each thrust became faster and deeper. He slid in and out of me, buggering me, sodomizing me... and I liked it. The pain had receded and a strange pleasure had overtaken me. I began to push back as hard as he was thrusting in. With every stab I pressed back more readily.

"Play with yourself," he ordered.

I didn't need to be told twice.

He kept on thrusting until my whole body jerked and convulsed uncontrollably as I climaxed. His cock swelled inside me as he too found his orgasm. Jet after jet of semen spurted into me while he held me tightly against his thighs.

27

REX

I was never one to appreciate waking up to a woman in my bed. As soon as I awakened, I wanted to jump out of bed and start my day, but here I was, spooning Willow without the least intention of getting up. I drew her soft, sweet-smelling body closer, and rested my hand on her flat belly.

She started to stir in my arms. I kissed the delicate skin of her neck. She was easily the most erratic woman I'd met in my life, but in a funny way, it was part of her charm. She was honest. No playing games, pretending to be coy. She said it like it was.

"Hey," she whispered, her voice heavy with the remnants of sleep.

"Good morning," I said, leaning forward to kiss her neck.

"Last night was great," she said, turning around to face me.

"Yes, you were fantastic," I agreed.

She stared at me with her large bottle-green eyes, and

without thinking about it, I kissed each eyelid. Something I'd never done to a woman before.

"How was the snake's stag party?"

I drew back. "God awful."

"Did he have strippers?"

"Of course, but have no fear, I behaved myself."

"I know," she said softly. "That's what I adore about you. Your word is gold. You said you were going to play the part of a perfect boyfriend, and you've done just that."

"You never really told me what happened at the alcohol-free hen party. When you came back you looked like you lost a hundred-dollar bill and found a dime."

"It was fine until Caroline said she had organized the hen party without my help." Willow's nostrils flared as she remembered the insult. "Can you believe that? Expecting me to help plan a hen's party for Tiffany after she stole my boyfriend?"

I chose my next words carefully. "I think you've made your point. Everybody knows you've got a new man who can't keep his hands off you. Why not try and enjoy the rest of the weekend?"

"I know I must seem like a mad woman with a vendetta to you, but I can't find it in my heart to forgive Tiffany, or Steven. I just can't. I've tried, but it's in my gut. Especially when I'm around her or my family, I can't help the pain I have in my chest. I can't explain it to you, and even if I did you won't understand it. As an outsider you probably think I have the perfect family and I'm just being a drama queen, but it's how it seems. Everyone in my family is pretending. I feel so abandoned, so alone. She has everything and all I've got is a boyfriend I've paid to act the part."

She looked so sad and lost, I wanted to take her away and protect her from her revolting family.

"No, I actually don't think you have the perfect family. I happen to agree with your assessment of Nicole and Tiffany."

Her eyes widened with shock. "You do?"

I nodded. "I think your stepmother is an incurable narcissist, and you must have had a very difficult childhood dealing with that level of manipulation. As for Tiffany, she's impossible spoiled and selfish."

"You know, Nicole did such a number on me, that I've sworn to myself never to be a stepmother. I'm terrified I'll be like her and ruin some poor child's life."

"You'd never be like her," I said sincerely.

"You know what they say about abused children, most of them grow up and take the first opportunity to become the abuser. What if I take all my repressed anger and hurt out on some innocent child? Nah, I'm never going to put myself in that situation. Never."

Willow pushed herself to a sitting position and swung her legs to the floor. "I better go get ready for the big wedding." She stood and went to the bathroom, shutting the door behind her. Moments later, the sounds of the shower filled the room.

I responded to emails on my phone while she showered.

The shower went off and five minutes later, Willow returned to the room, wrapped in a white towel. My cock lurched at the sight of her clear, cream skin and the just scrubbed look. Willow was one of those women who actually looked good without make-up.

I pushed aside the bed covers so she could see how hard she had made me.

"Wow," she said softly.

I wrapped my hand around the base of my cock and watched as Willow let the towel drop and sunk down, impaling herself on my erect shaft. Bracing her palms flat on my belly, she rotated her hips in slow circles around my cock.

I drove up, plunging my cock in and out of her. Willow met me thrust for thrust as hunger met hunger. We were both gasping for breath as we pummeled each other to the edge.

28

WILLOW

I got off Rex and lay down next to him. The high of the orgasm was gone and I suddenly felt exhausted. All the negative emotions and the extraordinary amounts of alcohol I had consumed in the last two days had finally got to me.

"What's the matter?" Rex asked.

"I'm going for a walk along the lake. My head's muddled. I need to think."

"Want me to come?"

I shook my head. He was part of the muddle. "See you when I get back, okay?"

He nodded. "Okay."

I got dressed and went out into the cold morning air. Immediately, I felt better. I kept walking in the cold until my thoughts became clear. I was not confused. I was in love. Oh God!

I was in love with Rex!

And I was dreading the end of the weekend.

I turned around and hurried back to the hotel. When I

got into our suite, I felt it instantly. He wasn't there. I ran to the table where breakfast had been laid out. There was a note there for me on the hotel's stationery.

Hey Beautiful,

Something urgent came up at work and I have to leave right away.

I'm so sorry I can't be at the wedding, would have loved to have stood next to you, but maybe it's not necessary. My job here is done.

I've already settled the hotel bill and instructed Solomon to book you transport to the airport. Please liaise with him about times etc.

See you on Thursday.

Take care, Willow.

xx Rex

For a second, I was so stunned I didn't believe what I was reading. Then I reread the note. Something so urgent came up on a Sunday at work that he had to leave without saying goodbye? Especially when he knew I'd only gone for a walk and would be back in minutes.

I didn't believe it.

I went through everything I'd said that morning to him. Did I say something to piss him off? I couldn't remember saying anything that would even remotely put him or anybody off? Then again, if he was upset with me why carry on with the meeting on Thursday?

I looked at the 'xx' before his name. Men didn't throw those around for nothing, did they?

I had no choice, but to take him at face value. I knew nothing about what he did for the company, but it must be very important, otherwise how could he put the bill for the Presidential suite down as a company expense?

Maybe something really bad did happen.

It was already nine thirty and I should be getting ready for the wedding. I went to the safe and to my surprise all the jewelry was still there. I felt sure then that he must intend to see me again. These pieces must be worth hundreds of thousands if not in the millions. The emerald necklace alone must be worth years of my salary.

I felt dazed as I got ready, slipping into my cream Chanel suit. It was a classic style. The gold buttons, embossed with the Chanel logo, gleamed in the morning sun slanting in through the tall windows. I put my hair up the way the hairdresser had shown me to and did quite a good job of it. Then I hung the pearl chains around my neck and slipped into the cream shoes that matched my suit. I looked in the mirror and I had to admit I looked amazing, but there was a terrible knot of confusion and shock at the base of my stomach as I left the suite.

Rex leaving so suddenly had thrown me for a loop.

My whole family was gathering in Tiffany's suite, but I was too tense to go there immediately. I decided to go down to Blackbeard's Bar. It was open all day, maybe I could get some Dutch courage first before I went up to Tiffany's suite.

As I suspected, The bar was completely deserted. I rang the old-fashioned bell, and a man popped his head up from behind the bar. He gave me a big grin. "Family of the bride, eh?"

I grinned back. "Yup."

"What can I get you?"

"Something with gin in it."

"Coming right up."

As I was waiting for my drink two men came in. They were wearing dark suits and looked like businessmen. One of them was talking loudly in a thick foreign accent. He could have been German.

"You know what America's problem is?" he asked.

Before the other man could reply he continued.

"America's problem is not Russia, Iran, China, or North Korea. America's problem is America. There is no outside enemy, my friend. There is only your own leadership that takes you into ruinous wars and has hollowed out your industries by sending them to China."

The bartender placed my drink in front of me and went to serve the men.

The man was still talking, but I no longer heard anything he was saying. I sat there stunned.

God, that was me. I was America.

There were no outside enemies, only me going on ruinous wars and hollowing out my own fantastic relationship with Rex by continuously obsessing about Tiffany and Steven. The God honest truth was, I didn't care one tiny bit about Steven so what did it matter if he wanted Tiffany? And as much as I hated to admit it, Nicole was right. Tiffany didn't steal Steven from me. Nobody can steal away someone that doesn't want to be stolen. Steven wanted to go with her.

He was wrong for me. He always was.

Why Rex even bothered to listen to me go on and on was beyond me. I must have been such a bore. I decided then, that I no longer wanted to punish Tiffany or Steven. Instead, I wanted to go to this wedding and be the bigger person. I wanted to wish them well with a sincere heart. In fact, I knew exactly how to show that I no longer carried resentment in my heart. I would go to the gift shop and buy something for the baby.

Leaving the drink untouched, I walked out of the bar. As I was crossing the lobby on my way to the giftshop, I saw Mrs. Dearborn hurrying towards me. I was feeling so good, I even felt a sense of familiarity and friendliness towards her.

"Oh hello, my dear," she gushed.

"Hello, Mrs. Dearborn."

She looked around. "Where is your charming man?"

"I'm afraid he had a work emergency and had to fly back early."

"Oh, what a shame." She dug into her handbag and fished out a small flat package. "I brought a slice of fruit cake for him."

Suddenly, I was filled with gratitude. Here was another person who knew and liked Rex. She was on our side. I reached down and, narrowly avoiding her large hat, kissed her on both cheeks.

"Oh my!" she exclaimed. "What was that for?"

"Giving you the kiss that Rex would have."

She beamed with happiness as I took the small package from her. "You will come back soon, won't you?"

"I hope so," I said a little sadly.

My time in this hotel had been magical, only I was so twisted up with bitterness, I couldn't see it.

29

WILLOW

I knocked on the door of Tiffany's suite and the door opened almost instantly.

"Wow! That suit is lovely, Willow," MaryBeth, a distant cousin said, with genuine admiration.

"Thanks, MaryBeth. You look lovely too."

"No, I don't. I hate my bridesmaid's dress. It's so ugly," she whispered fiercely.

I had to admit it was pretty ugly. Knowing Tiffany, she probably did it deliberately so none of the girls could ever even hope to hold a candle to her in the photographs.

"You look lovely nevertheless," I insisted. I lifted up the pretty paper bag I was carrying. "Now, where's the bride? I have a present for her."

"Come on," she said and led me to the main bedroom.

Tiffany was standing in front of a full-length mirror and a woman was standing behind her, fitting a veil on her tiara. I went closer and even though we had been lifelong enemies, I couldn't deny that she looked beautiful. Absolutely, fabulously, wonderfully beautiful.

"You look amazing, truly beautiful," I complimented softly. I really meant it as well.

She whirled around and met my eyes. Hers were cold and hostile. "What the fuck do you want?" she demanded aggressively.

Wow, she was not playing scared, helpless, poor Tiff today, then. The woman who was helping Tiffany with her veil tried to adjust it, but Tiffany knocked her hand away impatiently.

"Nothing. I actually came to say, I'm sorry. I've not been nice or kind to you these last two days. I was angry and hurt that both you and Steven had betrayed me, but I'm not anymore. I can see clearly now that Steven and I were never meant to be together. You and Steven are. He loves you and you love him. You make a wonderful couple. You deserve to be happy so I've come to wish you a very happy life together."

I held out the paper bag with the cutest tiny knitted yellow shoes inside it out to her. "This is for you. To say I'm sincerely and really sorry, and I'm really happy for you on your big day."

She snatched the bag, yanked at the tissue roughly, and fished out the little shoes. For a few seconds she looked at the shoes with something like disgust on her face, then she flung them across the room and looked at me with such fury I was shocked.

"I hate you. I really, really loathe you. You ruin everything. Everything. And now you've even ruined my wedding. Why don't you take a break from sucking his cock and go crawl under a stone and die?" she snarled viciously.

I stared at her in amazement.

"You think you're too good for Steven? You're giving him

away to me now like an unwanted hand-me-down because you think you landed the bigger fish?"

I shook my head in disbelief. "What? No. I'm trying to apologize for my behavior these past two days."

"Well, I got news for you, bitch. I'm not taking your left-overs. I too can find better."

"What about the baby?" the woman who was doing her veil asked in a scandalized voice.

"Fuck the baby," she shouted, her chest heaving.

We were staring at each other and the room had gone deathly silent when Olivia burst through the door.

"Oh my God, Willow," she cried, totally unaware of the hate and tension simmering in the room. "Why didn't you tell us who Rex really is?"

I had no idea what Olivia was talking about, but even if I did, I was too stunned by Tiffany's outburst to speak or respond.

"Who is he?" Tiffany shrieked. Her face was white and her whole body seemed to vibrate with wild animosity and rage.

"His name is not Rex Hunter. It's actually Rex Hunter Rothermere. He's the great-great-grandson of Arthur C Rothermere, you know, *the* Rothermeres, one of the richest families in the world."

My mouth opened with astonishment and a gasp of surprise ran through the room. Suddenly, Tiffany gave a screech of fury and pain and ran out of the room, her veil and long skirt flying out behind her.

"You didn't know either, did you?" Olivia asked.

I turned to look at her in a daze. She was wide-eyed with her news. "How did you find out?"

"The best man finally remembered where he'd seen Rex.

He'd been pointed out to him at an award ceremony. We went online to check it out and yeah, he's the real deal."

Nicole strode into the room, her face anxious. "What's going on here? Where's Tiff?"

"I don't know, she ran out of here when I told her about Rex," Olivia said.

Nicole glanced at me, her face unfriendly, before turning her attention back to Olivia. "What about Rex?"

"Steven's best man just told us all that he is actually a Rothermere."

"What?" she gasped, her eyes narrowing.

"Yeah, he's the great-great-grandson of Arthur C Rothermere," Olivia explained again.

Nicole turned to me slowly. "Clever girl. Very well played. Now what the hell did you say to my daughter to make her run away on her wedding day?"

"Nothing. I said nothing. I only came to say I was sorry for the way I've behaved in the last two days and to give her my best wishes for her wedding and her new married life."

Nicole's eyes narrowed. "You sly little witch. You made her feel small, didn't you? Now that you've bagged a man from one of the most famous families in the world, you've come here to brag and make her feel small."

"Mom, she didn't even know."

"Shut up, Olivia. You're a kid. You don't know her like I do." She walked up to me. "You came here with the intention of ruining that poor girl's wedding and you have. I hope you're happy now."

"I didn't ruin her wedding, Nicole, you did. If you had once in a while said no to her she wouldn't have turned out to be the spoiled, selfish, psychopath that she is now."

"How dare you?" she said, and slapped me so hard my

head swung to the side. I held my burning cheek and faced her.

"Good. You took your mask off. Finally, we can all stop pretending that we're one big happy family or that you're the perfect stepmother."

"Get out," she gritted between her teeth.

"With pleasure," I said, and walked out.

30

WILLOW

I cuddled Pogo in my arms and thought about my weekend.

My memories seemed almost like a dream. Did it really happen? Even Rex seemed unreal. A snowbound fantasy I had dreamed up in my head. I read his note over and over again. Always, my eyes went back to the two little kisses.

It had to mean something.

But now that I researched and understood who he really was it was starting to mean less and less. What would a man from one of the richest families want with me? Although, everything that had confused me before now made complete sense. No wonder he would never reveal even a little bit about himself, his family, or his past.

In the end it was all lies. Being a floating consultant, the hotel bill being put under expenses.

To think I bought his nonsensical claims about everyone doing him favors that would normally probably cost hundreds of thousands of dollars. The plane, the cars, the drivers, the jewelry, the clothes, the services of people like Nina, and the exclusive hairdresser she took me to.

God, I was so damn stupid!

No wonder Nina had looked at me strangely. She couldn't understand what I was doing with a man like him. Finally, the nonchalant way he left such expensive jewelry behind in the hotel safe for me to bring back made perfect sense.

The thing I truly did not understand was why?

Why did he take me on?

I simply couldn't comprehend why a man who belonged to one of the richest families in the world would agree to pretend to be my boyfriend for money.

The only slightly reasonable explanation I could think of was sex. Maybe he just wanted to sleep with me. But even that was silly bordering on ridiculous. A super wealthy, handsome, young man in his position could have any woman he wanted. He didn't need to play elaborate games just to get laid.

I offered one of the richest men on earth a thousand dollars for the job! When I remembered his expression that day I pushed the first check at him, I cringed at how dumb I must have looked to him.

"Oh, Pogo," I whispered. "What a naïve fool your mama is."

What next? He had left, and until now there was no phone call or a text, and yet he had specifically mentioned keeping the meeting with Olivia on Thursday. Since I believed his word was good it meant he really did intend to keep this appointment.

Would that night be the end of our relationship then?

When I looked in the mirror now, I even looked different. I was love sick and I didn't know what to make of everything that had happened. I went to work and got through the day like a robot.

Daisy, the busybody at work, told me I looked awful and asked me what was wrong. To close the conversation down I told her I thought I was coming down with something. But she immediately looked terrified and asked if it was Covid so I had to lie and say I'd tested myself and it was negative.

My phone pinged and I instantly picked it up and looked at it. My God! It was a text from Rex. I opened it with shaking fingers.

Hey gorgeous! Heard you had a good flight back.
Will send a car for you and Willow at 8pm tomorrow.
Let me know if that is not convenient.

For a long time I stared at the message, then I typed my reply.

That will be just fine. See you tomorrow.

After I clicked send, I phoned Olivia.

31

WILLOW

It was such a fancy French restaurant that Olivia was open-mouthed with wonder. We were escorted by a classically beautiful hostess to a secluded table in an alcove. Rex was not there yet.

"Remember not to mention that we know who he is," I reminded Olivia.

"My lips are sealed," she promised, looking around her curiously. "So, this is how the truly rich live."

"Olivia, you're supposed to pretend we don't know."

"I know that. He isn't here yet, is he?"

"Just get into character now, please."

She turned her face to my worried one. "Relax. I promise, you'll be shocked at what a good actress I am."

"Hello," a voice I both dreaded and longed to hear drawled from behind me.

"Hey, Rex!" Olivia squealed and jumped up to kiss his cheek. "It's good to see you again."

Rex looked at me. God, I had almost forgotten how

beautiful he really was. My body was immediately on high alert.

"Hello, darling," he greeted as he bent his head and kissed me full on the mouth. As if we truly were a couple. The way he slipped back into acting mode was so smooth and frictionless I stared at him with amazement. My mouth tingled and I could still smell his aftershave.

He sat down. "I hope Willow sent my apologies for leaving early."

Olivia looked at me then back at him. "Since the wedding didn't take place, I guess it didn't matter."

I watched Rex. He never reacted to the news that the wedding didn't happen. Either he was an amazing actor or he knew.

"How is Steven taking it?" he asked, as he signaled a waiter.

"Terrible. He's come around to our place twice in tears begging Mom to let him see Tiff, but Tiff won't see him. Mom felt bad for him so she told him Tiff might change her mind later, but no chance. Hell will freeze over first before Tiff changes her mind. She wants nothing to do with him. I think she plans to leave Bison Ridge and come to New York. She wants to start fresh."

The waiter appeared. "The usual, Monsieur?"

"Yes, and whatever the ladies are having."

"I'm just going to have water. I have to take the bus in two hours," Olivia said.

"I'll have whatever he's having," I told the waiter.

"Tres bien, Monsieur," he said with a respectful nod, and withdrew.

"Do you come to this restaurant often?" Olivia asked conversationally.

"Sometimes. The company has an account here so it's convenient."

"Will you be putting this dinner on the company expenses too?" I asked sweetly.

He smiled at me, but his eyes seemed to be drinking me in. "Not this one."

I stared back unable to move, hypnotized by his gaze. He looked away from me and turned his attention back to Olivia. "We should order soon if you have to leave in less than two hours."

The food was ordered, and Olivia raved about it so I guess it must have been good. They certainly looked like works of art, but to be honest I tasted nothing. I was too anxious and edgy. I listened to Olivia chattering about New York and how exciting it was, I heard Rex make his little comments here and there, and the whole time my stomach was in a tight, tense knot.

Eventually, after what seemed like an eternity, it was time for Olivia to leave. He had arranged for a car to take her to the meeting place she had arranged with her friend. I hugged her goodbye.

"It's all going to be okay. He's one of the good guys," she whispered in my ear.

Then she was gone and we resumed our seats.

"I've dry-cleaned the clothes that Nina let me borrow. Maybe you can get someone to pick them up."

"I don't think she'll be wanting those back. Just keep them."

Of course, she wouldn't. He had obviously paid for it all. I reached down to my bag and took out the flat package I had brought.

"The jewelry from the safe," I said.

"Right," he said smoothly, but he didn't make any attempt to take the package.

"I put the slice of cake that Mrs. Dearborn sent for you inside too."

His eyebrows rose. "She sent me a piece of cake?"

"Yup, it seems you've really impressed her. You've got a fan for life."

He grinned suddenly. "I hate fruitcake."

I didn't smile back. "I noticed you haven't cashed my check yet."

His grin died. "Yeah, I should get around to it. Been busy."

"Also, here's your bonus," I said, pushing the envelope with a check in it.

He frowned. "No. I left early. Keep it."

"No, you earned it. You went well and truly above what you were supposed to do. You deserve it. Just for the great sex alone, you deserve it," I insisted.

"I booked a room for us upstairs." His voice throbbed.

I stood. "Let's go then."

32

WILLOW

Rex kicked the door shut behind him, jerked me toward him and crushed his lips to mine. He bit my bottom lip and sucked my tongue like a starving animal.

Before my hands could even move to undress him, he'd already completely stripped me. Naked, he carried me to the bed and threw me down on it. I watched while he undressed and rolled a condom on. He got on the bed, grabbed me by my ankles and opened my legs wide. Excitement flared in his eyes as he stared down at my spread, wet pussy.

There was such hunger in his eyes. It was as if he had longed for me as much as I had longed for him.

A whimper of need escaped my mouth. God, how I wanted the feel of him inside me again. It felt as if years had passed since he was inside me.

He ran his finger along the slit of my pussy and put it in his mouth. He closed his eyes for a few seconds as if he was reconnecting with something he had missed greatly.

His thrusts were rough and fast, just the way I needed

them. I wrapped my legs around his waist, drawing him deeper into me. My nails raked his back. I lost track of time and place as each plunge took me closer to my orgasm.

I let out inhuman sounds, but it seemed beyond me to do anything about it. All I cared about was chasing that orgasm, which seemed out of my reach. Tears squeezed out of the corners of my eyes.

"Faster, Rex," I pleaded.

He obliged instantly, slamming into me, then lifting himself almost all the way out of me, and ramming it home again. His scent of pine and clean sweat was intoxicating. I clenched my teeth and half-rose as an orgasm crashed into me, making me scream like a mad woman.

"Fuck, you're even more beautiful than I remembered," Rex growled, just before he found his own release.

He lay next to me, breathing hard. We were both staring at the ceiling. Seconds ago, where he ended and I began, I couldn't have said, but now a chasm too deep to cross was opening up between us.

"When, if ever, were you planning to tell me that your real name is Rex Hunter Rothermere?" I asked.

I felt his body still.

Then he turned to face me. "How did you find out?"

"Steven's best man remembered."

"I bet that put the cat among the pigeons in Nicole's world," he commented cynically.

"Yes, it did, and it made Tiffany go into full Godzilla mode too. She actually screeched with fury and frustration."

"I'm surprised she didn't try to claw your eyes out."

"Too many people around, plus I'm taller and stronger than her." I paused. "When Olivia said the wedding didn't take place you didn't seem surprised."

"No, I wasn't. Tiffany told me she was having second thoughts."

"Really, when?"

"We bumped into each other while I was walking around the lake."

"Why didn't you tell me?"

"I thought you already had too much on your plate to contend with."

I frowned. "She told me to get your cock out of my mouth. Any idea why?"

His lips quirked. "I told her you gave the best blow job I'd ever had."

"What? Why were you talking about that with her?"

He smiled crookedly. "It's true... and I wanted to piss her off."

"Well, you certainly succeeded there." For a few seconds neither of us spoke. "Why did you lie about who you are, Rex?"

"I don't know. You wanted to pretend to be in a relationship and I wanted to pretend I was not a Rothermere. Just for one weekend I wanted to pretend to be an ordinary man. I couldn't resist the idea of going to a small town where no one knew me with a maddeningly sexy blonde."

"So, it was just a sex thing, huh? A dirty weekend with a dumb blonde that offered you a thousand bucks to pretend to be her boyfriend."

"No, I always knew you were not a dumb blonde. I wanted you the moment I laid eyes on you. You were so utterly different from the people I move with."

"Ah, you were slumming it?"

"Stop it, Willow. I wasn't slumming it. Nothing could be further from the truth. It might have started as a dirty weekend, but it's not that now. You are like a drug. My body craves you day and night. I can't seem to get enough of you. These last three days have been hell."

"So why didn't you call me?"

His face closed over and became secretive again. "Because I have something important to sort out."

"The same thing that made you leave Bison Ridge?"

"Yes," he admitted slowly.

"It's not work, is it?"

"No, Willow. It's not."

"Will you ever be able to tell me about it?"

"I'm working on it."

"So, what happens to... us in the meantime?"

"I want us to see each other, but not officially. Not yet. Just give me a bit of time, okay?"

What else was I going to say, but, 'Okay'.

33

REX

https://www.youtube.com/watch?v=Zi_XLOBDo_Y

I stared at the DNA results that my lawyer had delivered to my office. The child was definitely mine. My hands shook slightly. I was the father of a three-year-old boy. A boy I'd never met.

Never once in my life had I had sex without protection. And certainly not with Jessica. Unlike Willow, she was just pure fling material and never would have been anything more. I picked her up at a beach resort. She was working the bar. I remember her still. She had sad eyes and a firm body.

I thought about Willow.

I had to forget her for a moment and deal with the problem at hand. Jessica was sitting in a hotel waiting for the DNA results before we could talk. We hadn't met or spoken since I returned to New York. There had been nothing to talk about until the DNA results arrived.

Now, we had plenty to talk about, including why she hadn't seen fit to let me know I had a child all this time.

A knot of anger formed in my gut. That boy was my child. She should have told me. With every second, I grew angrier. I felt cheated. I grabbed my phone and called her.

"Hello," she said at the first ring, as if she had been staring at the screen, waiting for it to ring. "Rex."

"Can we meet?" I asked briskly.

"Yes. We can meet in the bar downstairs."

"Fine."

"I have someone minding Kayden, but it's nice to be nearby so you can see him," she said.

Kayden. That was his name. I took a deep breath. I really was a father. "Half an hour?"

"Okay," she said.

Finn drove me and stopped the car outside the bar. I expected to get there before Jessica as I was terrible at keeping time, but I found her already there. She waved at me from a table by a window.

"Rex." She stood up and made as if to hug me.

I stopped her with a look. I might have agreed to meet, but that did not mean I wanted anything to do with her. The four years since the end of our fling had not been kind to her. She had lost a lot of weight. Her face looked thin and pinched and her eyes seemed sadder than ever.

"Jessica." I nodded.

We sat down.

She smiled nervously and played with her fingers.

"Why did you wait all this time to tell me?" I asked. "And why are you telling me now?"

Before she could answer, the waiter came to take our orders.

"Nothing for me," I said.

"A glass of chardonnay, please," she said.

She hadn't been much of a drinker, which meant that the conversation we were about to have was making her very nervous. As it should. You didn't keep a man's child a secret from him. The waiter withdrew.

Jessica tried to smile and failed.

"In the beginning I didn't tell you because I thought you might either try to make me have an abortion or think that I wanted to use the baby to cling to you. I wanted the baby because I fell in love with you and wanted to keep something from you. And believe me when I tell you I would never have told you. We were happy together, Kayden and I. We didn't have much money, but we were happy." Her voice broke and she looked down at her tightly clasped hands.

The waiter brought her drink and set it on the table.

"So, what happened?" I probed.

Jessica looked visibly uncomfortable. "I met a man. He's different from you. He's not generous and... he... he is not kind to Kayden. He doesn't want Kayden. Michael wants us to have a clean slate to start from."

I was stunned. "What kind of sick people are you? What's wrong with you, Jessica? You'd give up your child to please a man?" I clicked my mouth in disgust.

"You don't understand. I love him." She grabbed her wine and drank it all in one long swallow.

I didn't hide my feelings. A woman choosing a man over a helpless child? Protective feelings rose inside me. I wanted that child away from her new man. A man like that was dangerous. He would make my son's life difficult. I wanted to take care of my own son.

"I want you to take him," Jessica continued, speaking in

a rush. "I've raised him for three years. Now, it's your turn. Besides, you're rich. You can give him the life I never could."

My body felt cold and my voice was chilly. "Are you willing to sign away your rights to Kayden?" Saying his name gave me the oddest sensation. Suddenly I couldn't wait to see him. Put my arms around his small body.

"Yes," Jessica whispered.

"Good." I called for the bill. "Where is Kayden now?"

"He's upstairs with my friend, Stacie."

"Does he know about me?"

"Yes, he knows you're his dad and I've shown him photos. He's excited. You can meet him now, and let me know when you want to take him home."

It felt almost overwhelming. He was only three years old. I knew nothing about three-year-olds. I didn't have tiny furniture for him.

She bit her lower lip nervously. "I understand it's an adjustment, but you'll manage. If you want, I'll help you hire a nanny and whatever else you need."

"Let's go," I said.

I followed her out of the bar into the hotel lobby. We didn't talk again even though we were alone in the elevator. My muscles were tight with tension when Jessica and I stepped out of the elevator.

Jessica stopped in front of a door and shot me a broken smile.

I didn't bother pretending to smile back. First, she had kept my son from me while it suited her, but now that she had a new man, her own child had become a burden to her and she wanted to foist the responsibility onto me.

She pushed the door open and stepped in. I saw Kayden as soon as I entered the room. He was on the floor playing with a set of trains and making vehicle noises. He looked up and when he saw his mother, a smile lit up his ridiculously cute face. The resemblance was unmistakable.

He looked like a mini me.

He stood up and ran to his mother, and with all the force of an NFL linebacker, wrapped his small legs around hers. A warm feeling spread across my chest and all of my body. I was only able to recognize it after a few seconds. It was love. I already loved the little guy. The love was fierce and protective. God help anyone who tried to hurt him.

"Hey, buddy," Jessica said in a soft tone that was so full of love it threw me.

I didn't get it. If she loved him so much, why did she want to give him away? I already knew that I was *never* going to give him up from that moment onwards. Not for anything or anybody. So, how could she do it?

Jessica unwound his limbs and he looked up at me, his eyes were my eyes. The same color, the same dark eyelashes. Jessica sank down until she was eye level with him. "Do you remember that I said we were going to see your daddy today?"

He stared at me solemnly, as he said, "Yes, Mommy."

My heart squeezed. As much as I wanted him to be mine, I didn't want to see him get his little heart broken when Jessica, the only person he had known and loved for three years, left.

"Well, here he is."

I smiled. A real genuine, full-of-love smile.

He gave me a tentative smile that slowly spread all across his face.

"Hi, Kayden," I said, a feeling of sureness coming over

me. Whatever happened, I was going to take care of him well. He was my own flesh and blood.

He moved away from his mother and came to me. His steps were tentative and yet fearless. I followed Jessica's example and crouched down. He stood close to me and openly studied me.

I cleared my throat.

"What did you do today?" I asked, figuring it was a good point to start a conversation.

"I played hide and seek with Stacie and I won," he bragged.

I chuckled. That's my boy. Winning from the age of three. I assumed the youngish woman who had disappeared through a connecting door when we entered the room was Stacie.

I couldn't remember ever being so enamored with a little human. I just wanted to keep talking to him.

"What did you eat?" I think I just wanted to hear him speak. For reasons I could not explain, I wished that Willow was there to share the moment with me. To meet my son. To share in my joy.

He took some time to think about what he ate, and when he answered he gave me a precise answer, detailed to the number of peas he had eaten.

I laughed. "Do you always count all the peas you eat?"

"Yes. Mommy said I have to eat at least ten," he informed me solemnly.

"Ten is a good number. That's why you're growing to be so strong and healthy."

Kayden abruptly raised his arm to flex it and I saw a large bruise on the inside of his arm. The fury that coursed through my body was such, I had clenched my hand into a fist so the kid would not see me angry and become scared of me. I knew where he had got the bruise. I looked at Jessica.

"You're a natural," she said.

I touched the bruise. "Where did this come from?"

She looked sad then. Really sad. "That's why he's coming to live with you."

I let my anger go. "He looks well. You've done a good job raising him."

"Thanks," she said, sorrow in her voice. "He's an easy boy to love."

Yeah. Except for that asshole she had decided was the man she loved. But thanks to him, I was getting a chance to get my son back. I shuddered when I thought of what might have happened had he wanted to raise Kayden as his own.

I would never have known the kind of love I was feeling.

Afterwards, I said goodbye to him, promising to return the next day. Jessica walked me to the elevator. We agreed that she would give me a day to organize myself.

"I've compiled a list of everything you'll need to get for him and also his routines. He hasn't started school yet so you're free to choose the school you want him to go to."

I knew nothing about schools, but Kayden would obviously go to the best school.

As I turned away from Jessica she started to cough, but she coughed in a way that made me turn back and look at her. There was blood in her handkerchief.

"What's going on, Jessica?"

"The big C got me," she said with a weak attempt at dark humor.

"What?"

"Yeah, it's one of these new aggressive cancers apparently. It started off at stage four. I have, at best, a few months left."

I stared at her. No wonder she looked so ravaged and now that I looked properly, I saw that she was wearing a wig. "You have to have a second opinion. I'll arrange for you to be seen by the best oncologist in New York today."

"No, Rex. No. I'm not doing the chemo thing again. It nearly killed me the first time. I've made my peace. Now that I know Kayden will be safe with you, I'm ready to go."

"Is there anything I can do for you?"

She shook her head and smiled. A big smile that came straight from her heart. "You've already done it."

As I rode the elevator down, I felt a strange mixture of sadness and elation. I felt sorry for Jessica, but Kayden was now mine. All mine.

My heart pounded erratically when I saw a message from Willow. She wanted to go out for dinner. I would have loved to have said yes, but I needed time to think.

I had to find a way to make Willow accept that Kayden and I came as a package even after she had clearly, with heartfelt emotion, sworn she would never allow herself to be a stepmother.

34

WILLOW

"I guess, since I can't go to your place, you should come back to mine, instead of spending a fortune on hotel rooms," I suggested.

Rex looked amused. "Don't worry about it, Willow. I'm just calling in a favor."

"Yeah, very funny. But seriously, what a waste of money."

"Your place is too far from your workplace, or my home. It makes more sense for us to meet in the middle."

"Where do you live?" I asked curiously.

"Steinway Tower, 57th street," he said.

Of course, he lived a stone's throw away from Central Park on the street called the Billionaire's Row.

"It won't always be like this," he added softly. "Just give me a little time to sort my situation out, okay?"

"Are you... are you ashamed of me, Rex?" I asked.

That expression of indulgent mild amusement fled from his face. "Oh, Willow. Never. Nothing would give me more pride than to take you to meet my family."

I frowned. "Then what is it? Can't you just tell me?"

"I will tell you. Just not yet. Maybe, if I can get it all to fit, next week."

I sighed.

He angled his mouth over mine and when our lips touched, a moan escaped my mouth. Oh God. It was only one night of being apart, but how had I gone on for so long without him? He tasted of heat and wine—a heady combination. Our tongues swathed over each other, teasing, tasting.

Rex 's hands roved over my back and ass and I did the same. Our movements grew more frenzied. Then Rex pulled back, lifted me up and carried me to the bedroom.

He kissed me again then moved down to cup my breasts and kiss my nipples. I let out a luxurious moan. Pleasure pulsed in my veins and my pussy throbbed with the need to be possessed.

He pushed my knees up and wedged himself between my thighs. First, he teased my folds with the tip of his cock, then he pushed his cock in, plunging deep. I let out a cry and clung to his shoulders as he thrust in and out.

I came quickly as if I was having sex for the first time.

Sweat clung to both our bodies as Rex kept up the rhythm. In and out. In and out. He let out a low rumble of pleasure as he came, his cock filling my pussy with hot cum.

35

REX

What I was doing wasn't fair to Willow, but she belonged with me and so did Kayden, so come hell or high water I would find a way to persuade her to accept my son.

Willow was a warm, loving woman, and Kayden was irresistibly adorable.

There was no way she would not fall immediately and completely in love with him when she met him. I was sure of that. I just needed to get all the pieces in order before I introduced them.

I drained my coffee just as Finn texted to let me know that he was waiting downstairs. I left quietly making sure not to wake Willow up.

First things first. Kayden.

Just thinking about him brought a smile to my face. My son. Unbelievable that a blood connection could change my life just like that. Make me smile for no reason whatsoever.

The day was jam-packed with stuff I had to do to bring him over to live with me.

In the morning Jessica and I interviewed several live-in nannies, before we settled on one. A sweet woman in her late twenties who had worked with children all her adult life. Hannah had a gentleness about her that made me instantly trust her with Kayden.

In the afternoon, Jessica helped with furnishing Kayden's bedroom and all the other stuff that a three-year-old needed. It was amazing how such a small person needed so much. I might have overdone the toys, but seeing the joy in his eyes when he opened them. Pure joy.

What really helped was when he met my Swiss Shepherd dog. I didn't know how Shadow would react to a baby and I had him on a leash, but the connection was instant. Both were utterly fascinated with each other. Shadow licked his chubby hand and Kayden threw his arms around Shadow's neck and laughed with delight.

Then Jessica left and it was just me, Kayden and Hannah. Kayden didn't seem bothered that his mom had gone. She'd promised to visit in two weeks though.

The first night, I was nervous as hell, but having Hannah around helped. She was awesome with him and after the first night, I felt a little more confident about my role as a dad.

Willow and I exchanged a few text messages, but I told her I was swamped with work. I felt guilty that I was lying to her, but I promised myself that when things settled down, I would explain everything to her.

We would then open a new chapter in our relationship.

Kayden was the easiest little boy to take care of, even Hannah said so. Soon, she said, a routine will settle into place and things will get even better.

The first thing I did when I woke up at dawn was check

in on Kayden. I'd left the door half open, so I tiptoed in. He must have been tired, because he was sound asleep half-covered by the comforter.

Shadow trotted to me from the other side and proceeded to lick my legs. He'd already given himself the role of Kayden's bodyguard, following him all day.

I stroked Shadow for a few minutes, pulled the comforter around Kayden's little body, and stood watching him sleep. With a smile, I left his room.

Hannah, it seemed from the sounds coming from her end of the corridor, was already up.

"Morning," she said when I walked into the kitchen. She was dressed a lot differently from the way she had until now. A pair of tight white shorts and a crop top.

"Good morning," I said, trying to figure out the appropriate dress code for nannies. No idea, but I was pretty sure that those shorts were not part of it.

"Coffee?" she asked with a smile that bordered in flirtation.

"Sure." Maybe I was overreacting. It was Friday after all. A lot of people saw Friday as the beginning of the weekend. She poured me a cup of coffee and rather than slide it across the island, she came around to my side.

She brushed against my shoulder with the side of her breast. It wasn't my imagination. The nanny was trying to seduce me. Fuck. How had I not seen this coming? I took a sip of my coffee and kept my face impassive. Under normal circumstances I would have gotten rid of her, but the last thing Kayden needed was more change, just when he had gotten attached to her. If I utterly ignored her unsubtle advances she would get the message, especially once I introduced Willow into the picture. Time would take care of her infatuation or whatever it was.

"I was thinking of taking Kayden to the park at lunch time," Hannah said. "He'd like it if you joined us, even if just for an hour?"

"Fine. I'll be there. Text me the time." I drained my coffee and excused myself.

I peered into Kayden's room just as he was waking up. He sat on his bed and rubbed his eyes.

"Morning, buddy," I said, walking in. I lifted him out of his bed. His little body was warm from sleep.

"Morning, Daddy," he said, melting my heart.

I still hadn't gotten used to being called daddy. I wanted to hear it over and over again. Was it the same for all parents? For Kayden, our relationship seemed natural to him. As if I'd been in his life from day one. I kissed his forehead.

"I'm going to work now, but I'll meet you and Hannah in the park."

He beamed. "I like the park. Will you push me on the swing?"

"I sure will," I said and ruffled his hair. Kissing him again, I left feeling as if I'd left a part of myself behind. I had no idea what kind of life he'd had with his mother and her man but I was going to provide for him the best lifestyle I could. He would lack for nothing.

"Morning," I said cheerfully to Finn, as I slid into the car.

He turned to me in surprise. "Morning, Sir."

It dawned on me that I wasn't a morning person. Or I hadn't been. Finn and I never spoke in the morning in the past. I grinned. One could not be grouchy with Kayden in one's life.

He dropped me in the basement of the building. My usual steps were to take the elevator that took me straight to the executive floors. On a whim, I took the stairs to the first floor, wanting or needing to see Willow before I started my work day.

I ignored the stares that followed me as I cut across the open plan office to Willow's desk. Her face was set in concentration, her eyes on the screen in front of her. I sat down and studied her. Today, she had worn her hair in a ponytail.

My fingers itched to undo the ponytail and thread my fingers through her hair. The background noise of typing fingers and muted conversation faded. All I was aware of was Willow. I caught a whiff of her signature perfume, reminding me of how she looked when she first woke up. I'd missed that.

Her gaze left the screen. She gasped and her hand flew to her chest. "Rex, you gave me a fright."

I chuckled. "Sorry. I should have said something, but it was more entertaining to stare at you without your knowledge."

She wagged a finger at me but she was smiling. "You've been busy."

"I have," I said and got more comfortable on her visitor's chair. She looked over my head and back at me. "How about dinner today?"

"You beat me to it. I was coming to invite you for dinner."

We agreed that I'd pick her up at home at half past six.

I whistled as I went up the elevator towards the executive suites. Life was good. "Morning, Phyllis," I greeted Larry's secretary.

Her eyebrows flew into her hairline. "Morning, Mr. Rothermere."

At lunch time, Finn drove me to the park. Since I got there before Hannah and Kayden, I picked a bench where I had a view of the entrance. A few minutes later, Hannah and Kayden strolled in, hand in hand. I stood up and almost instantly Kayden saw me. He grinned and took off on a run in my direction.

I squatted and he flew straight into my arms.

"Daddy," he said, burying his face in the crook between my shoulder and head.

"Hey, buddy," I said, emotions choking me up. I had no idea what I'd done to deserve him in my life, but I was going to do my damn best raising him.

Since he was dressed warmly, we decided to visit the animal zoo in the park. We bought food from a dispenser to feed the animals. Listening to Kayden's shouts of glee as a goat ate directly from his hand turned me to mush.

"He's so sweet," Hannah said, coming to stand too close.

I stiffened. "Yes." I answered curtly to discourage conversation.

She got the message because she did not speak again.

We bought some sandwiches and milk for Kayden and sat on a bench to eat. Hannah made some small talk that included Kayden, but generally she behaved impeccably in front of my son.

36

REX

"Play with me some more, Daddy," Kayden said as I stood up from the floor where we'd been playing with his firetrucks for the last half-an-hour.

I kissed his forehead. "Do you remember I told you I have to go and meet someone?"

He nodded, but he didn't let go of me. Kayden was not clingy at all so the fact that he was clinging worried me. Conflicted, I picked him up and held him close. He wrapped his hands around my neck and laid his head on my shoulder.

My throat choked up. We stayed that way for several minutes until Hannah gently pried him away from me.

"We'll be just fine. I can play with you," she said firmly.

I shot her a grateful smile and left.

Finn opened the back passenger door when he saw me. "How is the little man doing?" he asked with a smile.

"He didn't want me to go," I said, glad to talk about Kayden with anyone. I'd tried calling Jessica a few times but she didn't answer her phone and the one time that she did, she sounded rushed.

"They never do," Finn said. "But if you look inside the window right now, I bet you he's playing happily with his nanny."

I nodded. Finn was probably right. I turned my mind back to Willow. What was the plan? I didn't have a plan. For the first time in my life, I had no detailed plan. All I knew was that I wasn't going to give her up. No matter what.

Finn cruised to a stop outside her building and I texted her to let her know I was outside. I got out of the car to wait for her. She emerged, looking gorgeous.

"Hi," she said and went on tiptoe to kiss me. "Your skin is cold. You stood in the cold waiting for me?"

"You look beautiful," I murmured, her scent hanging in the air around me. God, I'd missed her.

"Thanks," she said and slid into the car.

I'd made reservations at a Mexican restaurant, but to my disappointment the atmosphere wasn't the quiet dinner I had envisioned. There was a large party celebrating something and our table was next to theirs. I asked for another table but the restaurant was full.

"It's fine," Willow said. "We can still hear each other speak."

"If we shout," I said.

Willow laughed. "But I like shouting."

And just like that I knew I loved her. I stared at her with wonder. Yes, I was crazy in love with her.

"Why are you looking at me like that?"

"Because you're breathtakingly beautiful."

She blushed. "I'm not."

"Yes, you are, you're even more beautiful than my dog,

and he's a beauty, easily the most beautiful dog in the world."

"You have a dog?" she gasped.

"Yes, a white Swiss Shepherd." I wished I could talk to her about Kayden, but not just yet.

"Will my Pogo get to meet him?" she asked.

"If you can get him to leave his hiding spot behind the curtains," I commented.

She laughed. "Oh, how did you know about that?"

"You told me that while you were drunk our first night at The Lake Club."

"How embarrassing, I can't remember telling you. Yes, Pogo is a little monkey of a dog. My neighbor came over yesterday and he wouldn't come out to say hello. He suffers worse mood swings than a woman."

I laughed as she regaled me with new tales of Pogo. Her dog had character. Kayden would love him. I could just picture him crawling all over the house playing hide and seek with Pogo and Shadow. I quickly checked my phone for messages from Hannah. Nothing. That meant all was well.

The waiter returned with our wine and the food menu.

"How do you feel about children?" I asked casually, after we'd made our food selections and we were alone again.

She looked surprised by my question. "I don't mind them, I guess. I don't know. I've not been around children much, but I guess I do want them... one day." She shrugged. "For the moment, I'm happy with Pogo, just as you're happy with Shadow."

My chest tightened with disappointment. I'd made the right call in not telling her about Kayden yet. He was my responsibility and I didn't want to make Willow feel as if she had to be a certain way because I suddenly had a child. She hadn't signed up for this. I had. I had to find a way to get her to fall in love with Kayden, the way I had.

My phone vibrated with a message. At this time of the night, it could only be Hannah. I touched the screen. It was Hannah.

I don't want to worry you but Kayden is a little hot. I'm keeping an eye on him. Will let you know if we need you.

A little hot? What did that mean? I texted back.

Does he need a doctor?

"Is everything okay?" Willow asked.

"Yes, yes, everything is fine," I assured her, but I couldn't stop worrying about Kayden. I glanced at my phone every few minutes.

"Should you be somewhere else?" Willow asked, one eyebrow arched.

"No, sorry." I wasn't convincing. Ignoring the glass of wine, I signaled to the waiter and asked for water.

Hannah texted again twenty minutes later.

I think he does need a doctor. Definitely a fever.

I excused myself, headed for the washroom, and arranged to meet a doctor at home. Back at the table, I asked for the check then turned to Willow. "I have to go. Something urgent has come up that I need to take care of."

"The same reason you had to leave Bison Ridge?"

I nodded.

She looked crestfallen, but she didn't pursue the matter

further. While I drummed my fingers impatiently against the door handle, she was quiet on the drive home. When we reached her apartment, I walked her to the entrance of the building.

"No point in inviting you up, is there?" she said, as we stopped outside the entrance.

"Not tonight," I said. "Let's do this again tomorrow, okay?"

Her eyes flashed. "Okay. Goodnight."

She entered the building and I sprinted back to the car, my heart pounding. *Please, please let him be okay.*

I FELT like a complete asshole as we drove home, but Kayden's health had to come first. He needed me. Still, that didn't get rid of the guilt. The hurt look in Willow's eyes haunted me.

We got home in record time and as soon as the car stopped, I raced in. The housekeeper told me that the doctor was in Kayden's room with Hannah.

"How is he?" I asked, entering the room like a hurricane.

"Nothing to worry about. It's just an infection," the doctor informed me, and quickly explained that it was a common thing with children before their immunity fully developed.

"Hey, Champ," I called in a cheerful voice.

He looked at me with listless eyes. "Where's Mommy?"

"Mommy's away, but I'm here for you, okay?"

He nodded. "Okay. Can you ask her to come tomorrow?"

"She's on holiday, Champ. We don't want to spoil her holiday by asking her to come back, do we?"

He shook his head, his face serious. "No. No, we don't."

It tore at my heart to see him like that. I asked the doctor tons of questions, and by the end of it I was convinced that Kayden would be okay. He was given a painless injection and a liquid medicine to take for the next few days. Hannah walked him to the door and I stayed with Kayden until he fell asleep.

I left his door slightly ajar and headed to the kitchen.

"Do you want some coffee?" Hannah asked.

"Yes, please," I said and gratefully sat on a bar stool. How the hell did parents raise children without dying from worry? The evening had been the longest of my life and Kayden was not even seriously sick.

"He'll be fine," Hannah said as she set a mug on the island in front of me. "It will happen many more times."

"Don't say that." I took a sip of my hot coffee. "I don't think I can handle many more of these incidents."

Hannah smiled. "You will. Sorry I interrupted your dinner."

I didn't want to think about Willow and how she had interpreted the evening. Whatever she was thinking was wrong and I couldn't even tell her that. "It's fine."

"Oh, and Jessica called," Hannah said. "She wanted to speak to Kayden, but I told her that he wasn't feeling well."

That was odd. She rarely called, and the timing could not have been worse. I finished my coffee and checked on Kayden. He was sleeping peacefully and the fever had definitely gone down.

Jessica called again at seven in the morning. "What's up?"

"I'm leaving today," she whispered. "Michael is taking

me home for a few days, then I'll be checking into a hospice."

I didn't know what to say. "Do you need money, Jessica?"

"No, I don't." There was a pause when neither of us spoke. Then she carried on in a hush voice. "I wanted to tell you something, something I never thought I'd tell anyone. I know you will be angry when I tell you, but I'd like to get it off my chest before I die. May I?"

"Of course," I assured, gripping the phone tighter. I hoped and prayed it was not going to be something bad about Kayden.

"I wanted you to know that Kayden was always wanted. He was never, not even for a second, unwanted. I wanted him before he was born, before he was even out of your body."

"What do you mean?"

"I pricked all the condoms you left on the bedside table while you were in the shower. All of them. And before you left for the weekend, I replaced the unused ones with new ones so you wouldn't get anybody else pregnant by accident."

I couldn't believe my ears. "What? Why?"

"Because I knew from the first moment I laid eyes on you that you were the man I wanted to have my child with," she said simply. "And now that I have told you, I can die peacefully. And one more thing. I have no regrets. Not a single one. I'd do it all again, given half the chance."

She made sniffing sounds and I could hear that she was crying. "The only true pain I have is being parted from Kayden now, when I need him the most. But I know he's in safe hands. And that's all that's important."

How strange life was. I had been so furious with her and

now all I felt was pity and sadness for her. “First of all, I’m not angry with you, not anymore anyway. You can’t be angry with the person who gives you the greatest gift you’ve ever had, and secondly, he is in safe hands, the safest possible.”

“Thank you. That means everything to me. Please take good care of him. He is my heart.”

“I will. You have my word on that.”

37

WILLOW

"Hey, how about dinner and drinks?" Melissa asked.

We were the only ones left in the office. Everyone else had closed up for the day. I quickly glanced at my phone. Nothing yet from Rex. I swallowed down the sigh that was working its way up my throat. Something was going on with him.

He had changed in the last few days.

He'd become cagey.

Wednesday was the last time we'd been together. As usual, he'd rushed home after dinner as if someone was waiting for him. I hated the insecurity and the fear that had come over me. What if it was Steven all over again? What if he was cheating on me? I'd been so sure of him, but what did I really know about him?

No, I told myself sternly. I wasn't going down that road. He probably had things going on at work and so far, he hadn't given me a reason to mistrust him. Wanting to rush off back to his own place and not inviting me was not a sound reason to think that someone was cheating. Especially, when he had expressly explained that he had some family thing going on and needed a bit of time.

"You're overthinking it," Melissa said. "It's just dinner and drinks."

I let out a laugh. "Sorry, I lost my train of thought. Yeah, I'd love to." I turned off my laptop and cleared my desk.

"Let's try this new place on Fourth street."

"Sounds good to me."

The new place was a restaurant with a lively bar. We were lucky to get a table for two considering how busy it was. I looked around, loving the frantic atmosphere and the happy chatter of people having fun. Living alone meant that you were surrounded by silence a lot, especially during the weekend.

I checked my phone again. Nothing. It was Friday. Why would Rex not call or text?

"You could just call him yourself," Melissa suggested.

"What?" I asked, heat creeping into my cheeks.

"The way you keep checking your phone means there's someone you're waiting to hear from. I've been there," she said in a kind tone.

I nodded, relief flooding me. I desperately needed to hear someone's opinion. "He hasn't called to make any plans for the weekend," I said and then told her how odd he'd become.

"There could be a very simple reason," Melissa said.

"Yeah, like what?" I asked, genuinely perplexed.

Our attention was taken by the waiter bringing our drinks.

"I don't know but why not just show up at his place?"

"No," I said horrified, remembering that he had clearly

said he was not ready for me to visit him. To turn up unannounced would be too stalkerish.

Melissa lifted her cocktail and sipped at it while staring at me over the rim. "Why not?"

"I can't go without letting him know first. He's not ready for that. It's invasive for me to just turn up without an invitation," I said.

"Hell, girl. You're too soft. No man is gonna see the inside of my panties unless I see where he lives first."

I let her words settle inside my brain. Why couldn't I go to his place? See for myself what was going on. Unease gnawed at me. It felt wrong to just go to his place. I had never been the kind of woman who looked through her boyfriend's phone or pockets. Maybe I should have been. I could have saved myself two years of being in a rubbish relationship. I took a large sip of my wine, forgetting what I'd told myself about taking it easy on the drinks.

"I'm telling you; you have to go to his place."

I inhaled deeply. Did I really want to go to such lengths? I recollected how the last few days had been. I had to ask him a few times if he was okay. Of course, he maintained he was and yet I knew without a shred of a doubt something was very wrong. "Maybe you're right. Going to his place is one solution."

"It's the only solution," Melissa insisted. "You can go after we eat."

Over dinner, I kept checking my phone, hoping that Rex would text and save me the trouble of going to his house unannounced. What if I turned up and he was in bed with another woman? My knees knocked against each other under the table. No. He wouldn't.

I didn't think that was his style.

Besides, he didn't need to keep me in his life. All he had to do was end things with me. A memory popped into my mind of a conversation we'd had along those lines. Rex claimed that he had never and would never cheat on anyone. His view was, if you have to cheat, you're in the wrong relationship anyway, and you should end that one immediately and go for the other one. Remembering that relaxed me somewhat and I managed to convince myself that there was another explanation for his odd behavior.

"The gentleman at the bar would like to buy you ladies a drink?" the waiter who had been serving us said.

Melissa and I exchanged a glance before turning around to look at the man in question. Not bad looking. He gave a small wave, but his eyes were on Melissa.

"Sure," I said quickly before she could refuse. Despite Melissa's brave talk, she wasn't the same when it came to talking to men. I gave the waiter our order for drinks.

"What are you doing?" Melissa asked, her voice shaky. Gone was the confident advice dispenser.

"He likes you and he's cute. You're not taken, are you?" I asked, knowing full well that she was single.

"Well, no, but I'm not ready to date yet."

"What's wrong with you?" I asked bluntly. "A hot guy buys you a drink and you're not ready to date? Who said anything about dating? It's just a drink. Relax."

She laughed suddenly. "You've seen right through me. You're right. It's just a drink."

I convinced Melissa that we should move to the bar. The man who had bought us drinks made a spot for us and introductions ensued. His name was Jared and he was clearly very interested in Melissa. That lessened my guilt when I left twenty minutes later.

I fidgeted in the Uber as my mind went back and forth. Twice, I came close to asking the Uber driver to drive to Manhattan. Then I chickened out, went home, and climbed into bed with Pogo. I shouldn't let Steven turn me mistrustful of all men. Rex was not Steven.

He specifically told me to wait. And wait I would.

38

WILLOW

Of course, I had every intention of waiting for him to invite me to his home, but somehow, I found myself walking in Central Park, then past Todd English Food Hall, and without really noticing, I was strolling along the exclusive Billionaire's Row. My heart was racing as I stood on the street opposite his apartment building.

I felt like a stalker.

It was a horrible feeling. I hated it.

Disgusted with myself, I was just about to turn when the doorman opened the door and a woman and a child came out. I think the thing that caught my attention was that the woman was nothing like the glamorous type of woman I expected to live in a place like that. She was young, and not bad looking, with a killer body. Even though it was cold and I was bundled up in a thick coat, she was dressed only in a tight-fitting dress that showed off her great figure.

"Hannah?" the little boy called.

I shifted my gaze to him and it hit me straight away. He

was a mini version of Rex. A gasp escaped my mouth. I turned to stone as Rex appeared behind them.

"Come on, guys," he said.

Nausea rose up my throat. I stood frozen on the spot in disbelief. Rex was cheating on me! And not just cheating. He had a child as well. He was playing happy families behind my back. I staggered back and the movement must have caught the corner of his eye because his head whirled around in my direction.

"Willow," he uttered. His face was white with shock. Obviously, he had never imagined I would show up unannounced.

I raised a hand in the air. "It's okay. I'm just sight-seeing."

Then I turned and fled, running as if I was in a flight for my life. Oh God. Oh God! What a fool I was. The pain that started in my chest was spreading to the rest of my body. What was the matter with me? You would have thought that after Steven I'd learned my lesson. But no, of course not. I had to fall in love with the next man who gave me a bit of attention.

I desperately needed to be alone. To think. To actually process what I'd seen.

I became aware of Rex's footsteps on the sidewalk gaining ground, and his voice. "Willow, stop. It's not what you think," he shouted.

That stopped me in my tracks. Burning anger coursed through me. It was one thing to be cheated on and another to be turned into a fool. I whirled around and faced him. My chest rose up and down as I gasped for air.

"It's not what I think?" I sneered. "Really? That's what you're going with?"

"Listen to me—" he began.

But I cut him off. "Is that why you've been keeping me away from your house?"

A gust of cold wind blew hair into his eyes and he pushed it aside impatiently, before nodding. "Yes."

That rendered me speechless. I'd expected some form of denial. To my horror, tears sprouted in my eyes.

"That boy is my son. His name is Kayden," Rex said, speaking fast. "And the woman is his nanny. Her name is Hannah."

I stared at him, wanting so much to believe what he was saying. I said the first thing that popped into my head. "Why is she dressed like that if she's a nanny?"

He let out a frustrated laugh. "I don't fucking know. When we interviewed her, she dressed nothing like she is these days. I just ignore it because she's very good with Kayden. I figure she'll get tired of it when she sees it isn't working. Willow, listen, a woman could walk around my house naked and I wouldn't be interested if that woman was not you."

"You said, we interviewed, who's we?" I whispered.

He frowned. "Kayden's mother and I."

"Where is she now?"

"With her man."

A shaky smile pulled at my lips. "Really?"

"Really. Now, come on. I want to introduce you to Kayden, then I'll tell you how he came into my life."

It dawned on me just how many secrets he had been keeping. "And why didn't you tell me all this?"

He sighed. "Because I only found out about his existence while I was at Bison's Ridge, and I didn't tell you because I was in shock. It was too much even for me to process. Then when I did process it all, I found it hard to tell you, because I didn't want to put you off. You didn't seem too anxious to be around children."

"I said that?"

"Yes, you did. At dinner, the Mexican restaurant," he reminded.

"Oh, that!" I said airily. "I was a different person then. I've changed a lot since that day."

He took my hand. "My God, your hand is frozen. Come on, let's go back up to the apartment and warm you up."

I was shaky but oh so relieved as I followed Rex. The nanny and Kayden were standing by the entrance staring at us.

"Hannah, this is my girlfriend, Willow," Rex said, holding my hand.

Hannah smiled, but it did not reach her eyes. "It's nice to meet you."

I was used to that and I understood exactly what was going on. She had seen an opportunity. A single dad and a billionaire to boot. I was going to have to get used to women making eyes at Rex. If I turned myself upside down every time a woman made eyes at Rex, I was going to be a very unhappy woman.

I turned my attention to Kayden. He really did resemble his dad. Instinctively, I crouched down to his level.

"Hi," I said.

He smiled shyly.

"I'm your dad's friend. My name is Willow."

"Willow," he repeated. "Like the tree?"

I smiled. "Exactly like that."

"It's Mommy's favorite tree. She said it looks sad."

Rex signaled to a burly man in dark jeans and a leather jacket who was standing a few feet away. "Follow them to the park," he instructed. Then he patted his son's head. "Ray will push the swing for you today, okay?"

"Okay, Daddy," the boy agreed easily.

The three of them left and Rex led me into the foyer. Another man came into the elevator with us, so we didn't speak. I just pressed myself against Rex's hard body and reveled in the wonderful warmth that came from it.

The condo was breathtakingly beautiful with long walls of glass that looked over the park, but I couldn't appreciate it. I needed answers. There was so much I wanted to know. What was really going on? Where had Kayden come from?

Rex rang a bell, and a woman appeared.

"This is Mrs. Wells, my housekeeper. Mrs. Wells, this is my girlfriend, Willow Garrett."

"Nice to meet you, Miss Garrett. Can I get you something to drink?"

"Uh... no. I don't think so. Thank you."

"Bring us a bottle of red wine anyway," Rex said, and Mrs. Wells departed.

Happy butterflies flitted in my stomach as I watched him. I suspected that he felt the same because he stopped in the middle of the room and just smiled.

I was glad that I'd followed Melissa's advice, else I don't know how long we'd have gone without Rex ever telling me what was going on in his life.

"You look so beautiful," he said.

"Thank you." I felt as though I was floating on air.

39

REX

https://www.youtube.com/watch?v=x-skFgrV59A

I made myself sit down next to Willow rather than toss her over my shoulder and carry her to my bed. Seeing her, inhaling her scent, made me more aware of how much I'd missed her in the two days. I'd been running out of excuses and I was glad that everything was out in the open.

"He's an adorable little boy," Willow said.

"I think so too," I said.

Mrs. Wells came in with the bottle of wine, which she proceeded to pour into two glasses. As soon as she left, Willow reached for her wine and took a sip. Then she turned to me. "Let's start from the beginning, huh?" There was a lot of hurt in her voice and I felt like crap because I'd put it there.

The only thing that would do was honesty. "Jessica contacted me when we were at Bison Ridge, or rather she contacted my people. She said that I was the father of her child, and she wanted to leave the boy with me."

Willow's eyes widened but she didn't say anything, allowing me to continue with my explanation.

"Anyway, I got back and the first thing we did of course was the DNA test. It came out positive, but even without it, one look at Kayden and I knew that he was my son."

"Why didn't she tell you before that?"

I explained everything to her and Willow's hand had flown to her mouth, covering it.

"That's insane," Willow said.

I'd kinda gotten so used to the circumstances surrounding Kayden coming into my life that I'd forgotten how truly shocking and unbelievable it would be to a lot of people.

"So yeah, that's how I ended up with Kayden. I was furious with Jessica to start with, but without her, I'd not have Kayden. She has already signed over her parental rights to Kayden. All she wanted was visitation rights but that won't be for long either. She'll be moving into a hospice soon."

"Wow! Poor thing. What an amazingly selfless sacrifice she made to give Kayden up to you now, so he would not see her suffer and die."

Over the years, I'd listened to parents go on and on about the kind of love they had for their children, but I had never understood the all-consuming nature of having a child. You couldn't if you were not into children in the first place or didn't have kids. Now, I understood. I also understood why Jessica had given up Kayden too.

Willow shook her head and stared at something in the

air. “Well, I think he’s a lucky little boy to have you in his life. From what I’ve seen so far, you’re a wonderful father.”

“Thank you. He’s really important to me and I want to give him a wonderful childhood to make up for his lack of a mother.”

She bit her lower lip. “You know when you asked if I wanted children, I thought it was just one of those questions people throw around casually. If I had known that you had Kayden, my answer would have been very different. I really didn’t mean to imply that children are a burden or anything like that.”

“I should have given you a chance and told you the truth about what was going on, but I think I’m still not totally sure it’s all real. Everything happened so fast. I haven’t even told my parents.”

I closed the distance between us, took her wine glass and set it on the coffee table. I slid my hand at the back of her neck. “I’ve missed you.”

The air between us became charged with sexual tension. Willow slid onto my lap and wrapped her arms around my neck. Her breath fanned my face but all I cared about was tasting her sweet lips.

“I’ve missed everything about you too,” Willow said in a husky voice.

She brushed her lips against mine and heat spread across my chest. I probed her lips open and slipped my tongue inside her mouth. She tasted of red berries and sunshine. On a cold day, it made me crave her taste.

I growled when our tongues found each other. After that I was lost and had to have her right there and then. “Let’s go to my bedroom,” I said to her. I didn’t want any interruptions. I stood up and Willow wrapped her legs around my waist.

I carried her to my room, deposited her on the bed and made sure to lock the door with the key.

Draping my body over hers, I continued where we'd stopped, hungrily sucking, biting and tasting. My erection pushed into the apex of her legs. She moaned as she raked her fingers through my hair.

I drew back and pushed up her blouse and lowered my head to tease her nipples through her bra. Willow's soft moans filled the room. She half sat up and unclasped her bra, tossing it to the floor.

My mouth wandered away from her nipples, trailing my way downwards to her flat belly. I pushed her skirt up and bunched it around her waist.

"I can't wait to taste you," I muttered, pulling her panties to the side.

Willow raised her hips, bringing her pussy to my eager mouth. I clamped my mouth on her pussy and blew. She pulled a pillow over her face and made muffled tortured sounds that fed my pleasure. I couldn't get enough of her sweetness and her response.

I pulled the pillow away. "The room is soundproof."

I fired off short little licks and sucks and her moans became a desperate whimper. Pushing my fingers inside her pussy, I flicked her clit and pumped my fingers in and out. I knew she wouldn't last long.

I was proven correct when less than a minute later, her whole body clenched and she screamed as her orgasm hit full force. She was panting hard while I licked her clean. Standing up I pulled down my pants and boxers. I was so hard, it actually hurt. Then I was back on the bed in between Willow's open legs.

She folded her legs back to her chest and spread them, showing me her wet, soaking pussy.

"You're so fucking sexy," I said to her, pushing my erection into her slick opening.

I closed my eyes as Willow's wet heat enveloped me, gripping me tight as I pushed my cock deeper and deeper. She was deliciously tight. I fucked her in a slow rhythm, needing to pleasure her once again before I came.

"Oh God, Rex," she moaned, her lips remaining slightly parted.

I loved the sound of my name from her mouth. That was all I needed to know that I was hitting the right spots. Every time I pulled out, her pussy tightened around my cock, milking me and taking every ounce of self-control that I possessed not to come there and then.

I alternated between fast and slow thrusts. Willow kept up with me, then she was urging me to move faster. I obliged, feeling as though I would lose it at any moment.

She came with another loud groan and I held back no more. I gave in to the pleasure that was waiting impatiently in the wings. Later, Willow lay in my arms. It felt so right and so perfect. I stroked her hair and her back.

"That was something else," I said.

"It was," she said with a sigh. "Hey, what's the etiquette for sleeping with a single dad?"

I laughed. "Is there etiquette?"

"There must be. I can't walk out of your room in the morning like I used to. We wouldn't want Kayden to see me," Willow said, real concern in her voice.

I loved her for it. "Kayden is three. He'd probably think I have a new roommate."

Willow laughed. "Maybe so, but I still don't want him to see me leaving your room. I'll leave before he comes back home."

"No, stay the night and have breakfast with us," I said, not ready for her to go.

"Okay," Willow said and yawned. "Sorry, it's been a long day and I walked the park and the street for hours before I picked up the courage to come and stand in front of your building."

"It's fine." I kissed her forehead. "Nap for a while."

I waited for Willow to fall asleep then I went to the bathroom. Afterwards, I slipped back into bed and lay down, content to just stare at her as she slept. My goal right now was to raise Kayden well and to have Willow by my side, but Willow was still an unknown in my happiness equation.

That thing she said about not wanting to be a stepmother made me feel uneasy. She had been so empathetic about it. It was something that came from deep within her. From years of living in a fucked-up relationship with her stepmother.

40

WILLOW

I glanced at the time and turned off my laptop. As soon as I placed it on the table, Pogo moved from my feet up to my lap and stared at me.

"Hey," I said, massaging the folds around his neck. He made purring noises and stretched out his body. "Your life is much simpler than mine." I really needed to get up and get ready for the zoo date with Rex and Kayden.

Kayden really loved the zoo. Apparently, Rex had taken him twice already, and whenever he suggested a different activity, Kayden insisted on the zoo.

Since the nanny had the weekend off it would just be the three of us. Not that she gave any problems at all. After the introduction of me as Rex's girlfriend, she had gotten the message and had started wearing clothes suitable for the cold weather.

I had an hour and a half before they picked me up. I quickly tidied the house and did my laundry, then jumped into the shower. A glance outside my bedroom window told me that it would be another cold day so I opted for a chic cream cardigan that went down to my knees and a pair of leggings. A scarf and a beanie completed the outfit. At a few minutes to two, I made my way downstairs to wait for Rex and Kayden.

I spotted Rex's car down the street and followed it as it purred to a stop. Rex rolled down his window, grinned and waved. Kayden did the same from the back passenger side. I laughed and waved back.

I hurried to the car and entered the front passenger side. "Hi."

Rex leaned in to kiss me on the mouth and my cold lips instantly heated up. "Hey, beautiful."

I turned to Kayden and he grinned at me. Kayden was such a sweet child.

"Hello, Willow Tree," he sang.

"She's not Willow Tree. She's just Willow," his father corrected.

"No," I protested. "I like being Willow Tree. Let him call me that."

"Don't teach him bad manners," Rex said with a laugh.

"No, let him live in his child's fantasy world. He won't be three forever. You think he'll be calling me Willow Tree when he's twenty?" As soon as I said the words, my heart lurched. Would I really be in Kayden's life then? That would mean... I'd be his stepmother. I pushed the frightful thought away. Later. Later, when I was alone, I would think about it again. Reaching out I gently tugged at his nose, making him laugh.

"So, what are we going to see in this zoo?"

"My goat," he announced proudly.

"Oh, you have a pet goat at the zoo?" I asked, intrigued.

For the rest of the ride, Kayden regaled us with tales of

his goat, most of which were obviously made up, but Rex told me that the goat in question was real though.

Rex and I couldn't help laughing at Kayden's antics. Kayden brought out a childlike, fun side to our relationship. At the zoo, we went straight to the goats' section and Kayden pointed out his black and white goat.

"Does he have a name?" I asked him.

He nodded. "Yes. It's Billy."

When he looked away, Rex and I exchanged a look. My heart skipped a beat just from locking eyes with Rex. I was in trouble. I was so deeply in love with Rex that no matter how much I told myself to take it easy, it didn't work.

The zoo was fun, especially watching Kayden's face light up when an animal came out of its hiding spot. I had a feeling he and Pogo would hit it off. Afterwards, we had a light lunch at the zoo restaurant, then we headed back to Rex's apartment.

Kayden fell asleep on the way back.

"Hey, you're awfully quiet," Rex said. "Did we wear you out?"

I grinned. "Never. I'm okay, just enjoying the drive."

"Then you'll be disappointed because we're home," Rex teased.

We trooped into the house with Rex carrying Kayden. I went to the kitchen and made some coffee for us. I carried the mugs to the living room and settled down on the couch. My feet had started to hurt from all the walking we'd done.

As if he could read my mind, Rex lifted my feet and massaged them.

"That feels so good," I said with a sigh.

"Did you enjoy the day?" Rex said. "I know going to the

zoo would not be your first choice of fun activities for the weekend."

"I loved it," I said and laughed. "Kayden is a fun little guy. You're very lucky to be his dad."

"I know. Are you serious that you enjoyed it?" he insisted.

I nodded. "I did. Kayden is special."

Rex's hands stopped their hypnotic massaging and there was something in his eyes. Something that made butterflies flutter in my stomach. Was he thinking about us parenting Kayden together? Being a family? I didn't want him to say the words. Not when I wasn't ready. Once the words were out, they couldn't be taken back.

I grabbed my purse and fished for my phone. "I should call for an Uber ride."

"Hey, what's going on?"

"Nothing, but I just remembered I have some work I need to finish." Not the best lie, but it was the best excuse to leave that I could come up with at that moment.

"What? I thought you were spending the night?"

I couldn't look at him. If I did, he would see the fear in mine. The fear that I would do wrong by little Kayden. Luckily the Uber driver called me to say that he was outside Rex's gate.

"I can't, I'm sorry." I shot to my feet. "The driver is waiting." I grabbed my weekend bag from the table at the foyer and literally ran out. I couldn't even begin to imagine what Rex was thinking. But whatever it was could not be worse than him knowing the truth. That I was afraid I would make a terrible stepmother to his beloved son.

I was glad that he had not followed me.

I got into the Uber and as I fastened my seatbelt, I felt

sick to my stomach. When the car dropped me off at home, I popped into the neighbor's apartment and picked Pogo up, before I went to my own place. I'd never been so grateful to be home. Even Pogo caught my emotions because he wouldn't leave me alone. He followed me to the bedroom and curled up with me on the bed.

I let the tears come then.

I cried until I had no more tears. I kept wondering what Rex was doing. So much for a weekend together. I was glad that I'd kept my mouth shut and not told him what had been on my mind.

I'd promised myself to stay away from my phone, but I had to check if he'd tried to call me. He had. Five times and texted a few messages.

I don't understand what happened. Talk to me Willow.

Are you okay? Did you get home safely?

If you don't text back, I'll send someone to check in on you.

I hurriedly checked the time of that message. Ten minutes ago. I texted him back. The last thing I wanted was to have someone who was not Rex come and check up on me.

Me: I'm okay. I fell asleep.

Rex : Why couldn't you fall asleep here?

Me: Told you. Work.

Rex : Will we see you tomorrow?

Me: Yes.

41

WILLOW

The first thing I did when I woke up was reach for my phone. Rex had not texted again. Disappointment crashed into me.

"What do you freaking expect?" I scolded myself. "You walked out of there with an obvious lie for an excuse, what else was he going to do? Keep begging?"

I got up to feed Pogo then jumped into the shower. Until Rex called, the day stretched out ahead of me, and not in a good way. I ate fruit for brunch.

While I was cleaning up my dishes, the doorbell rang.

Rex.

I was so happy I felt almost dizzy. Wiping my hands on my jogging pants, and checking my reflection in the mirror by the hallway, I hurried to the door and hit the buzzer, releasing the lock for the entrance door. Thank God the house was neat. Still, I fussed with the seat cushions until I heard footsteps. I flung the door open with a huge smile on my face.

"Tiffany?" I blinked rapidly, sure that my brain was playing tricks on me.

She let out a strange laugh. "Hi."

"What are you doing here?" I tried to act like I was not bitterly disappointed but I was. I stared at her closely. Her eyes were bloodshot as if she had been crying. Then I noticed the bag that she was carrying. *What the hell?*

"Can I come in?" she asked in a small voice.

I didn't really want to invite her in, but curiosity got the better of me. I stood to the side and shut the door after she entered. Pogo came tearing towards her, growling and barking like a mad thing.

"Sorry," I said, as I scooped him up and took him into the bedroom. I kissed him between his eyes and put him on the bed.

"Calm down boy. She's not worth having a heart attack over."

But he was not appeased. He jumped off the bed and tried to run back into the living room. Somehow, I managed to slip out.

I only noticed after I had sat down that we were both occupying more or less the same positions we had all those months ago when she came to my place to tell me she was sleeping with Steven.

"You're a long way away from home?" I observed casually.

Instead of answering, she started crying. I didn't know if it was her acting or she was serious, so I said and did nothing until she got control of herself and faced me.

"I just want to say, I'm sorry I went crazy that day. I know you were sincere. You really meant well. The shoes are beautiful." She started crying. "And my baby would have looked gorgeous in them if I had not had a miscarriage last week."

I gasped with shock. "Oh my God. I'm so sorry."

She broke into fresh sobs. "I couldn't stay in Bison Ridge anymore. Everyone staring, pointing, and laughing at me."

I stared at her. I knew exactly what was coming.

"I know we never got on, but I want to try to be a good sister to you. I want us to be like the way you and Olivia are. Can I stay with you for a few days?"

I covered my mouth with both hands. "Look, Tiffany. To start with you can't stay with me because Pogo hates you."

"Well, can't you put him in a kennel or something?"

"No, I can't put him in a kennel or something. Anyway, I don't think we should immediately jump into being roommates. We can try to be friends first."

She frowned. "Where will I go then?"

"You can stay in a motel for the time being... until you find your own apartment."

"I don't want to stay in some flea-ridden motel. Can't you and Pogo stay at Rex's place and I can stay here until I find something?"

I shook my head in disbelief. Tiffany would never change. We would never be friends. Nobody could be friends with someone like her. She was so incredibly narcissistic. Everybody in the world was there just to serve and make her life better.

"No, Tiffany."

She chewed her bottom lip. "Then, maybe I can stay at Rex's place? I bet his apartment has loads of rooms."

I began to laugh. I laughed really hard. She was just unbelievable.

"Me being homeless is not funny," she said sulkily.

"You're not homeless. You have a home in Bison Ridge."

"I'm not going back there. Ever."

"Whatever. Do what you want, but you're not my problem. I'm not going to help you, Tiffany. You're going to have to do it all yourself if you want to live in the city. I had to find my own way."

She deflated like a pricked balloon. "I was so sure I could stay with you."

"Why? We've never been close. Actually, we were enemies for as long as I can remember."

"That's because I was jealous of you. I was jealous because your father loved you with all his heart and mine had loved me so little, he left without even a goodbye note."

I was surprised. That was probably the first honest and real thing Tiffany had said to me in all the time I'd known her.

"Look, I'm sorry about your dad."

"And you know what else? I wished my mother would have died like your mom. Then my dad would have come and got me and we could have started a new life somewhere else."

Wow! She was even more messed up than I imagined. She stood suddenly. "Anyway, I should go. I know when I'm not wanted."

"Where are you going?"

She shook her head. "I don't know, but I'll find something."

"Look, you can stay tonight if you're desperate. I'll take Pogo and stay at Rex's, but you have to sort yourself out tomorrow."

She gave an odd, almost maniac laugh. Like she had gone mad or something. "Thanks, but no thanks. I don't need your charity, after all. I'll find my own way. One day, I too will find a rich man, you'll see. I'll show you. I'll show you all."

Then she turned on her heel and walked out of my door. I stood in the middle of my living room, debating if I should call Nicole and tell her that Tiffany had been to see me. New York could be a dangerous place for a woman alone.

Then I left it.

My conscience was clear. I offered her a place for the night and she refused.

I had my own problems to take care of. First of which was to let that hound out of my bedroom. He was making an almighty racket behind the door.

42

WILLOW

We've got take-out and are coming to your place. Hope you like Chinese.

Before I could reply to the text, the doorbell rang. Just like him to send me a text when he was outside the entrance door of my building. I gave them a few minutes to ride up in the elevator, then opened the front door.

"Kayden," I called, and he ran to me. My heart melted as I hugged him back.

"Would you believe me if I told you I've missed you like crazy?" Rex said in a low voice.

I laughed, happy beyond words. His hands were occupied with bags, but he brought his face down for me to kiss him. I planted a very chaste kiss on his cheek.

"Where's Pogo?" Kayden asked, looking around my living room.

I'd told him about Pogo and how he liked to hide when I

had guests. "Probably behind the curtain. If you call him, he might come out," I said.

Rex looked around. "I like your place. Cozy."

"Small, you mean."

"No, it's cozy. I like a girl who buys a green couch."

"Hey, I love my green sofa."

"And I'd love to see you naked on it."

"That can surely be arranged," I said primly.

Kayden was making cooing noises next to the curtains while Rex and I went to the kitchen with the bags of food.

"Tiffany was here," I said.

Rex's face registered surprise. "Why?"

"She wanted to stay here with me."

His eyes widened. "Wow, that's a turnaround for the books."

"Actually, I felt quite sorry for her. She lost her baby."

Rex was quiet for a moment. "I'm sorry, but I don't like your sister. She's selfish and stupid, and she was never pregnant."

"What? How did you know?" I asked, astonished.

"She told me."

"When?" I demanded.

"When we were at the lake."

I shook my head in wonder. This was incredible news. The whole reason for the rushed marriage was for the pregnancy. "Wow, and you never told me all this time?"

"What good would it have done for you?"

"Why tell me now?"

"Because I don't want you to waste your pity on her. She is totally undeserving of it."

The more I found out about Tiffany, the more convinced I became that she was a headcase. Someone with no boundaries. What Tiffany wanted, Tiffany wanted no matter what she had to do to get it or who suffered in the process. No wonder he never fell for her 'poor me' act.

"You bought enough to feed an army," I commented, opening yet another container of delicious smelling food.

"I didn't know what you liked," he said simply.

I served the food onto three plates, and we carried the heaped plates over to the living room.

"I can't find Pogo," Kayden said from the couch.

"He'll show up once he knows he can trust you," I said.

We chatted as we ate. No one could tell that we had our differences the previous night. Rex and I felt perfect for each other.

"There he is!" Kayden shouted, startling all of us, including Pogo who promptly returned to his hiding spot.

"Oh, don't go, Pogo," he begged.

"He'll come back," I said. "Give him more time." I crossed my fingers that Pogo would come back.

After the late lunch, I left Rex and Kayden sitting in front of the television and went to make some coffee. When I returned carrying two hot mugs, I found Kayden petting Pogo. He looked up at me with triumph in his eyes, and I could see the same blue light in his eyes that I saw in his dad's.

"He came out," he announced proudly.

"I told you he would. He just needed to know that you're his friend."

Kayden had a thing with animals. They instinctively trusted him. I'd seen it at the zoo and now with Pogo. It took Pogo weeks to leave his hiding spot when there was a new face in the apartment.

"Have you told your parents about Kayden yet?" I asked, wrapping my hands around the hot mug.

"I'm telling them tomorrow and taking Kayden to meet them this weekend."

"Are they... um... a bit snooty, your parents? It's not an insult or anything, it's just with them being Rothermeres and everything."

He laughed. "No, not at all. You'll like them. They're down to earth people. My father broke off from his family before I was born because my grandfather didn't approve of his choice of bride. He wanted my father to marry into another banking family, but my father was in love with my mother, so he refused. My grandfather did the thing that very rich men do when they can't get their way with their children, he threatened to cut my father out of his will, but my father told him he would rather eat gruel with my mother than caviar without her. I believe it was the best thing my father ever did. He became his own man that day."

"So, you didn't have a billionaire childhood?"

"No way. When I was growing up, I had to earn every cent I got. I mowed lawns and finished the other kids' homework to make extra pocket money, but it was a good thing. It taught me the value of money and how to be self-reliant. Eventually, when my grandfather died, he left everything that had been meant for my father to me. If I had been spoiled as a child, I probably would have done what my cousins did. They blew whatever they could blow, and all that's left are the trusts that they can't actually touch. As for me, I tripled my fortune, and I'm going to teach Kayden those same lessons my father taught me about money and abundance."

Later in the afternoon I baked some chocolate cupcakes.

Both Kayden and Rex loved them. It was funny watching Kayden's face covered in chocolate icing.

Afterwards, the three of us spent the evening together until it was Kayden's bedtime and they had to go home. A feeling of sadness bubbled inside me as I watched them leave. I could have gone with them if it weren't for all these terrible thoughts swirling inside my head.

I liked Kayden, I really did, but could I be a mother to him? I thought about the selfless way Jessica had sacrificed her own happiness for her son's wellbeing.

Could I? Could I sacrifice like that for Kayden?

Until I knew I could, I couldn't be a mother to him. That would be unfair to him and to Rex. I knew firsthand how a stepmother could ruin a child's whole life, and I was not going to do that to Kayden.

43

REX

I spotted Matt at the counter when I entered our favorite bar. I clapped his back, pulled back a bar stool, and slid the wrapped package in front of him.

"What's that?" he asked.

"Homemade fruitcake."

He slipped it quickly into his jacket pocket. "Nice one. Now where the fuck have you been? It's like you fell off the face of the earth."

I laughed. "I've been distracted."

"By what? You're never distracted," Matt said. "Wait, it's not a woman, is it?"

Matt knew me well. We'd been best friends since college, then we started a company together and our friendship had been sealed for life.

The bartender walked to our end and asked me for my order. "I'll have the same," I said, pointing at Matt's beer.

"It is."

Matt grinned slyly. "Does this new woman have a name?"

The bartender set my beer in front of me on the counter. I reached for it, ignoring the glass and took a sip straight from the bottle. When I set it back down again, I found Matt looking at me waiting for an answer.

"Her name is Willow."

"Willow." He said her name slowly, as if tasting it. "Where did you meet?"

"Office party," I said briefly.

"I thought office parties were only good for a quick fumble in the broom closet."

"Things have moved on since then, Matt old boy."

"Shame. I liked my days in the broom closet with Elise Barbery."

"Elise Barbery. That's a blast from the past. Whatever happened to her?"

"No idea and I don't want to know. The past is best left in the past."

"Talking about the past, I found out I have a son."

Matt nearly fell off his stool. "You what?"

"Yup, I'm a father. Here, let me show you a photo," I said, taking my phone and scrolling through it.

"Hang on, hang on. Start from the beginning. When, how, what?"

I told Matt the story, and he shook his head in wonder. "Son of a bitch. She sabotaged your condoms. That's one dangerous woman, man."

Matt's attention was suddenly taken by something going on behind me. Almost immediately his features softened, and I knew who was behind me.

"Sorry, I forgot to tell you that Alice was joining us."

"Hi," Alice, Matt's wife, said, coming to stand between us.

"Hello gorgeous." I stood up and kissed her on the cheeks.

"It's been too long since I've had a drink. Mind if I join you two gentlemen?"

"Of course not," I said, moving up one space to make room for her between us. "How have you been?" It had been years since I had seen her, and I wondered what had made her come today.

"I've been fine, thanks," Alice said. We exchanged pleasantries, then Alice gave her order for a chardonnay.

"How was work?" Alice asked Matt and for the next few minutes, I listened as they exchanged highlights about their day.

A powerful longing came over me, accompanied by a feeling of loneliness. Work had always been enough for me. Accomplishing my goals had taken a lot of my time. Since Willow, work seemed a means to an end. It was no longer the end. Now the end had Kayden and Willow in it.

Looking at Alice and Matt, it hit home how much more there was to life. Willow's face filled my mind. Would we still be in love years from now? If the intensity of my feelings were anything to go by, hell yeah.

Matt jerked his head in my direction. "He's found himself a new woman... and a son."

Alice whirled around, her eyes wide with curiosity. "You have a child?"

Matt gave her the condensed version. "Yup. The kid is three years old. The mother only dropped him off now because she's dying."

Alice's eyes became even rounder. "Are you guys teasing me?"

"Nope," we both said at the same time.

"Okay, the mother is dying. So, who's the new woman then?"

"That'll be Willow," Matt said.

"Well, in that case you better bring her to dinner next week, then. And after that we have to meet your son."

44

WILLOW

I shrugged out of my jacket just as Melissa was passing by clutching a mug. The scent of coffee wafted up my nose and I decided my first stop would be the small kitchenette.

"Come join us for a drink after work," Melissa said.

My stomach muscles tightened. I wanted to say no, thank you, but I thought of my empty apartment with just my terrible thoughts for company. I needed to get out. To stop obsessing about Rex and Kayden.

"Sure, I'd love that," I said quickly before I could change my mind.

"Great. I'll tell everyone that you'll join us."

I headed to the kitchenette to make myself a cup of coffee. As I waited for the coffee to brew, I stared out the window at the rain that was falling steadily. My mind wandered to Rex.

~

"Hey, you ready?" Melisa asked a few minutes to five.

"Yeah," I said, trying to sound like I met friends for drinks every day. Shit, I'd forgotten how to do this.

I gathered my bag and together with two other women, we put on our coats and left the building. The bar was just down the block.

We found a nice table in the corner and sat down to order our drinks.

"I'm glad you agreed to go out with us," Melissa said as we waited for our drinks. "We've been speculating that you must have a demanding lover who doesn't want to share you with anyone."

Really, they were wondering about me. "What?"

Melissa chuckled. "There has to be a reason why you turn down everyone's invitation for a drink."

I laughed but did not directly answer her question. The waiter brought our drinks, which distracted Melissa from continuing with that line of questioning. The three were clearly good friends. I listened as they caught up with each other's love lives.

They were all dating regularly but none of them were in a relationship. It made me think of Rex.

"Thank you for coming out with us, Willow. You're not as stuffy as we thought you were," Lara said a couple of hours later with a giggle.

I laughed too, already feeling the effects of the cocktails I'd already drunk. "I'm glad I came too." My phone vibrated from the table, and I quickly grabbed it hoping it was Rex.

It was. I smiled foolishly as I read the message.

Hey beautiful. How was your day?

Nothing life changing but it warmed my insides.

"That has to be a man," Melissa said. "No female would make you smile like that."

I laughed, alcohol making me more unreserved than I normally would. "It's nothing serious. Just someone I'm messing with." I typed back a reply.

Out with friends. Thinking about you just now.

His response was immediate.

Oh yeah? What exactly were you thinking?

Ah. Not telling. *Wicked emoji*

Our phones were quiet after that, and I thought that my communication with Rex was over. The drinks kept coming and our voices grew louder. The girls talked about their plans for the holidays. Jenna said she was staying in New York as she didn't get along with her family.

I admired how casually she said it, without caring that she might look like a loser to everyone.

"You all don't know how lucky you are to have family," Jenna said, her voice slurring. She turned to me. "Especially you, Willow. You have family and a man. Your life is perfect."

My life was not perfect at all. I excused myself to go to the bathroom. I was drunker than I realized. My legs felt unstable, and I held on to the wall as I walked down the hallway. Shit. A splash of water on my face would do the trick.

I finished my business in the toilet and headed to the sink. After a few splashes of water, I felt marginally better. I dried my face and just as I was about to leave the bathroom, another wave of dizziness hit me. I backtracked and entered a toilet stall.

I put down the toilet cover, sat down and rested my head in my hands. Why the hell had I drunk so much? I wasn't much of a drinker, and I should have known better. The wave of dizziness started to recede, but in its place, a headache was taking root.

My phone chose that moment to screech from my purse. The temptation to ignore it was high, but the ringing tone was making my headache worse. I answered without checking the identity of the caller.

"Hello." My voice sounded like a truck had driven up my throat.

"Willow, is that you? Are you okay?"

I smiled despite the way I was feeling. "Rex! Yeah, it's me."

"Why do you sound so far away? Like you're in a hole?" he said.

A giggle broke out of me. "That's because I've locked myself up in the toilet. I might have drunk too much," I admitted.

"I'm coming to take you home. Where exactly are you?" he said.

I gave him the name of the bar, but as I started insisting that it was not necessary to come, he disconnected the call. Only after the phone went silent on me did I realize that maybe it wasn't such a hot idea to have him come after all. I looked like shit. Frantically, I tried to call him back.

The phone rang and rang. No answer. I left the toilet and even as I headed back to the bar, I hit call again, but Rex still didn't pick up. Should I wait for him outside? My legs were still wobbly, and I was lucky to make it back to the table without toppling over a chair or table.

"We were about to come and look for you," Melissa said when I sat back down.

"I was on the phone," I said weakly.

"Another round?" Jenny asked and the others said yes.

I asked for water. Before the drinks could even arrive, Rex was striding into the bar. He came up to our table, a charming smile on his face.

"May I borrow this young lady for a bit?" he asked, while helping me out of my chair.

All the girls were open-mouthed with wonder.

"Of course," Melissa said.

Rex held me up as we walked out of the bar. Not a word was spoken between us.

45

WILLOW

I let my head fall back on the head rest and closed my eyes. The dizziness was returning so staying still was no hardship. Rex only spoke once more to tell me he could stop anytime if I was feeling sick.

His cologne wafted to my side, making me want to curl up on his lap. I must have fallen asleep because the next thing I heard was Rex's voice.

"You're home, beautiful. I'll help you up to your apartment," he said, his tone brisk. He opened his door and closed it shut.

Ouch, even that noise hurt my head. What the hell was in those cocktails? I wondered if he was so irritated that he had had to come and fetch me. But that didn't make sense. He was the one who had offered. Insisted even. Or maybe he was disgusted at how I looked when I'd had one too many. I was sure that there were mascara streaks running down my face.

Misery came over me. I should not have answered his call. A drunk woman was not a pretty sight, especially me. I was known to say ridiculous things when under the influence. I decided I wasn't going to embarrass myself further by opening my mouth.

I bit my lower lip to ensure that no words left my lips.

Rex opened my door and helped me unbuckle my seatbelt. It felt nice to have my hand firmly in his, even though he was only doing it to keep me upright.

Rex opened the door and held it for me to enter, then followed me in.

"Can I get you a drink or coffee?" I asked him as I kicked off my shoes.

"No, I'm good. I have to go anyway. It's Hannah's day off and I called Mrs. Wells to keep an eye on Kayden," he said, his tone all business-like.

"Oh," I said. So, he couldn't wait to leave. "Thanks for bringing me home."

"You're welcome," he said, inching towards the door. He held the knob, then turned back to me. "What are you doing tomorrow afternoon?"

"I'll be home with Pogo."

Rex's glance bounced around the apartment. "Where is he?"

"He'll show himself when you leave. He doesn't do guests, remember?" I said with a laugh.

"Smart dog," Rex said. His gaze settled back on me, sending an electric current sizzling through my body. "Do you want to go to dinner with me and my friends, Matt and Alice, tomorrow?"

"Sure," I said, trying to sound cool.

"Okay." He smiled. Did he know how handsome he was? I doubted it. "I'll pick you up."

"Dress code?" I asked before he closed the door behind him.

"Casual," he threw over his shoulder and shut the door.

Pogo emerged from his hiding spot behind the curtain. I sank to the floor and sat cross legged. He came straight to my lap.

"Let's go to bed," I told Pogo, my good mood evaporating. I'd made an error of judgment when I agreed to go out for drinks with my workmates. I should have said no.

46

WILLOW

I stopped in front of him.

His gaze rippled down the lines of my body, lingering on my exposed cleavage. He traced a finger between my breasts and a shiver ran through me. My nerves woke up, demanding more.

"So, you took Kayden to see your parents, huh?"

"Yeah."

"How did it go?"

"It was love at first sight. My mother said it was like having me all over again."

"That's good," I whispered.

"You look ravishing," he said throatily.

"Thank you," I murmured.

Unable to resist him, I stepped forward and wrapped my arms around his neck.

Rex's eyes darkened. I pressed my breasts against his chest. He cupped my face and brought his lips to mine. A rush of arousal spread over every inch of my body as our tongues tangled with each other. Rex's hands cupped my breasts tightly, making me cry out in arousal.

Breathing heavily, I made myself pull back. "If we continue with this, we are not going to go anywhere."

Rex pulled me back into his arms and kissed me, stealing my breath away. "Why can't we just stay?"

I wanted to say yes so badly. "You promised to go."

Rex pulled down the straps of my dress to expose my bra. Then he pulled down my bra cups and lowered his head to my nipples and spoke to them.

"I promised to go, but I didn't promise not to be late."

"Just for a little while then," I said, arching my chest.

He teased my nipples, licking each in turn and biting on them gently. A moan escaped my mouth. It had been so long since we had been together like this. I placed my hand onto his neck, afraid that my legs would give way.

Shots of pleasure ran from my nipples to my pussy. I was going to have to change panties. They were soaking wet. Rex's hand slipped between my legs and caressed my wet pussy over my panties. I spread my legs further, giving him better access.

He dug his fingers under my panties and caressed my folds.

"Oh, Rex," I cried, grinding against his hand. I was so close to coming. He pushed his finger into my pussy and worked it in and out. I became a mad woman as an orgasm ripped through me, peaking and then bringing me down gently from that high.

It wasn't enough though. I wanted more of him. Not wanting to ruin my dress, I wriggled out of it and draped it over a chair. Rex sat down and pulled me to his lap. I straddled him and for the next few minutes we made out like horny teenagers.

"Are you on the pill?"

I nodded.

"I want to enter you raw, Willow," Rex said, his voice husky.

"I want that too," I said with a shudder.

He half rose and pulled down his pants along with his boxers, freeing his erect, big cock. Rex wrapped his hand around its base and pressed the massive tip of his cock to my entrance.

Lust burned into my brain and all I could think about was having that cock inside me, filling me, easing the deep ache I was feeling. I lifted my hips and with one hand on my waist, Rex guided me down to his cock.

I let out a moan as his cock pushed through my slick folds, forcing its way in.

"Oh God, Rex," I moaned as his naked thickness filled me.

I sat on Rex's cock. For a moment, we stared at each other. This was the next step. Our chests rose up and down. We had never had sex without protection, and it felt amazing to feel all the contours of his cock.

He gripped my hips and lifted me up, my pussy sliding up his cock. Slamming me down like I was a weightless doll, Rex moved me up and down his cock. I hung on to his muscular shoulders, letting myself drown in the sensations coursing through me.

Rex let go of my hips and brought his mouth to my nipples. I ground my sex against him as he pressed both my breasts together and sucked my nipples in turn. It felt like being showered with pleasure from all directions.

Suddenly, he moved away from my breasts and clamped on my hips again, taking back full control. Keeping his eyes on my bouncing breasts, he thrust in and out of me, while keeping me suspended in the air.

"Oh yes," I cried, as delicious friction penetrated every nerve. My eyes rolled back as I hurtled towards an orgasm. Unintelligible words left my mouth as I focused on chasing that orgasm.

I let out a cry as my body was gripped by a sharp pleasure that felt new and different. Frantically, I gripped his shoulders, determined to make the waves of my orgasm last as long as I could.

"You're so fucking sexy, Willow," Rex said, then he came in a hot rush of cream that filled my pussy.

47

REX

"I got a box of chocolates for Matt and Alice," Willow said as we drove to their house.

"You didn't have to."

"I know, but I wanted to. I hope none of them have an allergy. That would be a disaster."

"You're safe there. I've seen Alice eat chocolates and Matt can eat anything. He ate a cockroach for a dare once."

"Ugh, yuck. Pease, tell me something less disgusting about your friends," Willow invited.

I laughed. "Matt and I met in college, and he was already dating Alice then. We've been friends ever since."

"They must know you very well," Willow said.

"I guess they do. And vice versa."

Matt and Alice lived in a gated community and after going through security, the main gates slid open.

"This is beautiful," Willow said as she looked around in admiration. "It's the perfect place to raise a family. Do they have children?"

"No."

I slowed down and turned left to the drive that led to Matt's house. The houses were set back from the road, so you only caught a fleeting glance.

Eventually, the house came into view.

"Wow," Willow said. "This is the life."

I laughed at her honesty. Another woman would have pretended not to be impressed. "Yes, it's a lovely house."

We parked the car in front of the house and got out. The front door flung open before we reached it and Matt stood there grinning.

"Hey man," he said.

I introduced him to Willow, and he immediately folded her inside a big bear hug which made her laugh with a mixture of embarrassment and surprise. We followed Matt, past the living room into the open kitchen.

"Hi," Alice called cheerfully from the stove where she was stirring something. "Welcome." She wiped her hands on the apron and came to us.

I kissed her cheek and after introducing the two women, I gave her the bottle of wine and chocolates. "The chocolates are from Willow."

"Thank you, but you didn't have to," she said to Willow.

"I was brought up in a small town. That's what we do," Willow said.

After removing our coats, we sat at the island chatting as if we were all old friends. I watched Willow, how easily she blended in. When the food was ready, she insisted on helping Alice set the table for dinner.

Alice always held strong Christian values so after we sat down, we held hands as she said a blessing over the food.

Then we dug in, passing the dishes around until everyone was so full, we could hardly move. Matt got up to pour us a glass of wine, apart from his wife.

"What about Alice?" I asked.

They exchanged a look and then Matt reached for his wife's hand.

"No alcohol for the next few months for me," Alice said, her face wreathed in a big, happy smile. She looked up at her husband, then us. "I'm pregnant."

"Congratulations," I said.

"Oh, wow," Willow exclaimed. "How fantastic for you. I was just telling Rex that this was the perfect house to raise children."

"I agree," Alice said.

"How far along are you?" Willow asked.

"Two months. I just found out."

"Still early days," Matt said, a note of pride in his voice.

A longing for a family came over me. I imagined how it must feel to come home to someone who loved you. I shot an involuntary glance at Willow and found her looking at me, she quickly looked away when our gazes met.

We talked about the baby as we ate. Matt wanted a girl and Alice wanted a boy.

"So, how did you two meet?" Alice asked later as we relaxed after dinner.

I looked at Willow and we both laughed.

"Ah, you don't need to answer that question. I have a feeling it's not a story that should be told in public," Alice said with a laugh.

"It's not that bad," Willow said. "We met at the office party."

I looked at her. She looked so beautiful then. “But we could have met in the rain, under an umbrella.”

“We could have,” Willow said softly.

48

REX

"When will we see Pogo again?" Kayden asked me.

We were on the way to pick up Willow and go for lunch at Matt's house. Alice was captivated by the idea of Kayden and couldn't wait to meet him. Probably because she was pregnant, and their baby was a boy as well. A playmate for Kayden. Exciting stuff. Who would have thought that our conversations would be about our kids growing up as friends?

"Daddy?" Kayden called.

"Uhm." I searched my brain for what we had been discussing. Pogo. The plan had been to text Willow and let her know that we were downstairs. "Sure son, why not?"

I slid the car into a street parking space and turned off the engine. Kayden bounced up and down on his seat, impatient to get out. I unbuckled him and hand in hand we made our way to Willow's apartment building entrance. I hit the bell and a few seconds later, she buzzed us in.

I frowned. It wasn't safe to assume that you knew who it

was. I made a mental note to remind Willow that she wasn't living in Bison Ridge anymore. Burglaries in New York were as common as everyone knowing your business in Bison Ridge.

I carried Kayden as we entered the elevator. Willow was waiting by the door, looking gorgeous and ready to go.

"Hey, you two," she said with a huge smile.

Warmth spread all over my chest.

"Where's Pogo?" Kayden asked eagerly.

"Come in and say hello," Willow said. "He'll love that. He's missed you."

Before she finished her sentence, Kayden had shot past her into the apartment. Willow and I chuckled as we followed him in.

"He came out from hiding," Kayden said excitedly. Pogo jumped around barking and reveling in the attention he was getting from Kayden.

"I told you he missed you," Willow said.

Kayden grinned and went back to petting Pogo.

Willow was a natural with children. I pushed away the image of the three of us living together as a family.

We watched Kayden play with Pogo for a few minutes, then we left for dinner at Matt's home.

I PARKED the car and as we walked to the front door, Matt opened it.

"Whoa, who is this?" he shouted in a gruff voice while looking at Kayden.

"Kayden. I'm Kayden," Kayden shouted back.

"And I'm your ride," Matt replied, and lifting a squealing

Kayden high into the air deposited him on his shoulders. He began to do the elephant walk as he headed back into the house, and Kayden's delighted shrieks filled the air.

Willow and I were laughing as we walked in after Matt.

"Come on in," Alice said, meeting us in the living room.

I kissed her on the cheek and sunk into a chair. Matt settled Kayden down with toys which I'm sure they'd made a special trip to the toy store to buy.

"Wow, you're starting to show," Willow said to Alice.

An image of a pregnant Willow sprouted to my mind. She would look beautiful pregnant. I went as far as imagining my arms wrapped around her growing belly, before I stopped myself. What the fuck was wrong with me? My mind was going crazy imagining happy family scenarios when she hadn't made any commitments to me yet.

Alice rested her hands on her belly and glanced at Kayden. "I am, and we found out the gender of the baby. It's a boy."

"A friend for Kayden," Matt said, ruffling my son's head.

"That will be awesome," Willow said, but there was a forlorn note in her voice that made me turn to look at her.

We chatted for several minutes and then we moved to the dining room when dinner was ready. I was pleased to see there was a highchair for Kayden. I thanked Alice for it, sure it had been her idea.

Lunch was fun. Lots of laughter and remembering old stories. I was glad to see how well Alice and Willow got along. After lunch, we moved back to the living room, but I could see that Kayden was getting tired.

"Come and sit with me," Willow said to Kayden, and he went to her and laid his trusting head on her lap.

"Let me show you where Kayden can have a nap," Alice

said when she returned to the living room. “It’ll be more comfortable, and I have a baby monitor. We’ll know when he wakes up.”

Willow turned to me and I gave her a nod.

“Come on, little man, let’s go and take a nap,” she said to him.

And... just like that I knew. She would be the best mother for Kayden.

49

WILLOW

"You must be so excited about the baby," I said to Alice as I followed her carrying Kayden down the hallway.

"You won't believe how much. I'm so excited to be a mom, sometimes I don't sleep at night. I just can't wait for my baby to come out. I know, I know...it's months away."

"I'd be excited too." I laughed at her enthusiasm, but inside I felt sad. It was ironic how the world worked. I'd never met a man whose baby I wanted to have until Rex, and it was looking good. He was a single man until I met him and realized I was in love with him. Then suddenly, out of nowhere, he becomes a father, and complicates everything.

I let out a small, involuntary sigh of frustration, but Alice heard it.

"Is everything okay?" she asked.

For a flash of a moment, in that warm, friendly room, I wanted to spill everything to her, but I knew better. Even though she was kind and good-hearted she was Rex's friend, not mine. I didn't know her well enough to spill my guts to her.

"Oh yeah, everything's fine," I said, giving her a bright smile.

I turned back to Kayden. He looked sleepy but he wasn't asleep yet. "Want me to tell you a story?"

He smiled sleepily. God, he was sweet.

"I'll bring the monitor," Alice said and left.

"Once upon a time, there was a naughty snowman called Yadred. He had a carrot nose and two sticks for hands," I started in a soft, soothing voice. I'd come to love the days when I got to read for Kayden or tell him stories. I loved the way he slowly drifted off with a smile on his face. Heaven.

He made me wish he was mine.

Alice returned with the monitor and speaking in whispers, showed me how to turn it on, then left. I continued with the story and three minutes later, Kayden was deeply asleep. I kissed his forehead and tiptoed out of the room.

Matt's voice drifted to me as I walked down the hallway. Then I heard Alice's voice. My name was mentioned, and I found myself slowing down, then coming to a stop just before I entered the living room.

"When are you guys going to take the leap?" Matt asked.

My heart skipped a beat at the question. It was evident that anyone looking at us would immediately see how perfect we were for each other. I held my breath waiting for Rex's answer.

"What, marriage?" Rex asked.

"Yup. As far as I'm concerned that girl's a keeper," Matt said.

"I agree, Willow is awesome, and you guys are so perfect

for each other. In a way you never were with any other woman you've been with." There was a pause, then she spoke, "Anyone who didn't know her would think she's Kayden's real mother."

Guilt came over me as I stood there, my underarm dampening with nerves. I was eavesdropping, but I desperately wanted to know the answer to the question Matt was asking. Had Rex ever thought about marriage or a long-term relationship with me?

"Well, are you going to make an honest woman out of her?" Matt asked.

"You guys should learn to mind your own business," Rex mocked, but there was no malice in his words.

"Fuck off," Matt said.

"Fine, fine, be all secretive, then," Alice said, with a laugh.

I waited a few more seconds, made my expression neutral, then I coughed and entered the room.

LATER THAT AFTERNOON, as we were headed home, and Kayden was dozing in the back seat, I studied Rex's profile. He was so damn handsome. But more than that, he was good and loyal, and he made my heart do all sorts of crazy things in my chest. He glanced at me. "What?"

I inhaled deeply and arranged the words in my head. "Nothing. Just looking at a very beautiful man."

He grinned. "Kayden and I have a present for you."

"You got me a present?"

"Hmmm..."

"Why? It's not Christmas or my birthday."

Rex brought the car to a halt and turned to face me. His

expression was unreadable. "Do you only get presents at Christmas or birthdays?"

"Usually, yeah."

"Time to change that. From now on you're getting presents when you're good… and when you're bad, but especially when you've been very bad. In case you didn't notice, I like bad girls." His eyes glinted.

"Promises, promises," I said weakly.

I carried the shoulder bag which had Kayden's spare clothes. Hannah must have been looking out the window because the front door swung open before we got there.

"Hi, Kayden," she said. "I missed you."

"I didn't miss you at all," he confessed with a child's honesty, Hannah laughed.

"Well, in that case you better tell me everything you've been doing because it sounds like you had a wonderful time." She took his hand, and they entered the apartment together. She really was good with him.

"If you guys want an early supper, Mrs. Wells has left meatloaf in the oven," Hannah said over her shoulder.

If I wasn't in the picture, Hannah would probably resume her flirtation with Rex. With extra touches like making dinner and offering him an ear to listen to, Rex might be tempted to get together with her. I shook my head. What was I thinking? I didn't want to be that woman who was suspicious of every other woman.

The last thing I wanted was to be a version of my stepmother. She had ruined my life because she was so proud or pathetic, she married, then stayed with a man who wasn't in love with her.

"Hang on, Kayden. Do you want to give your gift to Willow first?"

"Yeah, I do," he said, and raced off to get it.

He came back with a gaily wrapped square box, which he held out to me.

I took it and shook it. Whatever was inside made soft thuds. I smiled at him. "Interesting."

"Open it," he urged, his hands clasped behind his back.

I tore open the wrapping, opened the box, and nestled inside black tissue was a white miniature of Pogo. My breath hitched. It was such a thoughtful gift for a little boy to give.

"I love it so much, thank you," I said sincerely.

"You're welcome," he said politely, but I could see he was pleased that I liked his present.

I bent down and kissed him.

"Right. You can go off with Hannah," Rex said.

They went away and I turned to Rex.

"Why do you look so beautiful and so sad?" he asked.

"I'm not sad," I denied.

He reached into his jacket pocket and fished out a small blue jewelry box.

"Is this for being good or bad?" I asked in a mischievous voice, because I was scared of the powerful emotions that were trying to overtake me.

"This is for things you haven't done yet," he teased.

I opened the box to reveal a delicate gold necklace. It was not the flashy stuff Nina and I had picked out. This was the kind of stuff a man gave a woman because he really cared for her.

A tiny gasp left my mouth. "It's beautiful." I looked up at him with tears in my eyes. "Thank you."

My brain screamed at me to throw myself at him and let him hold me until all these horrible thoughts inside me went away, but I couldn't.

"You're welcome, babe."

I turned around so he could fix the necklace around my neck. "Feel like dinner?" Rex whispered, his breath warm.

I turned my head and looked up at him. "No."

He gazed down at me, his eyes darkening. "My bedroom? I've wanted to have you to myself all day."

"Sounds good," I agreed, and led the way to his bedroom.

The sunset streamed in through the window, casting orange, red and yellow hues on the bed. Rex turned the key and then came and joined me on the bed. He stared deep into my eyes before he kissed me.

We made love passionately, intensely, and sweetly, and by the end of it, I had tears in my eyes. I knew I couldn't carry on like this. I needed some space to be away from him, to think and get my head straight again.

"What's wrong?" Rex asked, his forehead creased with concern.

"I need to go back to Bison Ridge."

"What?"

"Just for a few days. I need to think."

"Think about what?"

"Remember when you needed time to sort your situation with Kayden and I gave you all the time you needed without ever knowing what was going on?"

His face closed over. "Okay. I get it."

"Thanks, Rex."

"I'll get my secretary to book the Presidential Suite at The Lake Club for you."

I smiled sadly. "That won't be necessary. I'm not pretending anymore. What I am is what I am."

"You won't be pretending. You're my woman, and my woman stays at the Presidential Suite."

My chin trembled with the effort not to cry. I wanted so badly to bawl. No one had been so protective of me, since my father died.

"When do you plan to go?"

"Tomorrow."

"What time? I'll get the plane ready for you."

"Oh, Rex," My voice broke. "Don't. You'll just make me feel bad."

He looked genuinely perplexed. "Why would you feel bad because I want you to travel in comfort and not waste time with senseless rules and regulations at the airport?"

I pressed my lips together and nodded. "Okay. Okay. Thank you."

50

WILLOW

https://www.youtube.com/watch?v=j8fHNdrZTSI

It was so strange to return to the Lake Club without Rex.

I met Mrs. Johnson in the foyer. She tutted and went on about the big wedding that never was. She had heard that Steven was no good, and Tiffany had done the right thing to ditch him.

I wanted to laugh at the stories she was telling me. They were all lies, obviously spread by Nicole to save face, but I didn't. I said nothing, just nodded, and occasionally made some polite noises of agreement.

Upstairs, I leaned against the door, and it was like I could see the past as if it was a movie. A magical, elusive movie that would live forever in my mind. Rex and I, having breakfast, me trying caviar for the first time, us drinking champagne at the nest of sofas, having sex right there on the floor.

Slowly, I walked into the bedroom and stood in front of the big bed. I could see us, on top of the sheets, tangled and clawing at each other. I left the bedroom and walked into the bathroom. There I was, with my jeans snarled around my ankles, breathing hard, in a state of shock because I never knew, never dreamed, sex could be like that.

The doorbell ringing startled me out of my reverie. I went to answer it. Solomon stood outside.

"Welcome back, Miss Garrett. It's good to have you back," he said.

I experienced a strange feeling of affection for the stiffly polite man in front of me. "Hello, Solomon. It's good to be back."

"May I get you anything, Miss Garrett? Some champagne, perhaps?"

"No thank you. I'll call if there's anything I need."

"Please do, Miss Garrett."

I closed the door and suddenly, I couldn't bear the utter emptiness of the room. Without the larger-than-life presence of Rex, the suite was too silent, too hollow. There were too many ghosts here. I opened the door and looked out into the corridor. Solomon was just reaching the elevator.

"Solomon, um... could you arrange a car for me please?"

"Of course, Miss Garrett. Where to?"

"The cemetery."

He nodded. "The car will be waiting for you outside in five minutes."

"Thank you."

I went back inside the suite and stood by the door for about two minutes, then I left.

THE CEMETERY LOOKED ALL AT ONCE, lonely and magnificent. The ancient oak tree stood alone, its trunk gnarled and dark against the snow-covered land. I walked along the little path that had been meticulously cleaned by the old caretaker, Mr. Watcombe. A lone Robin-red breast followed me curiously, hopping on the ground a few feet from me.

Both my father and mother's graves were in impeccable condition. Nicole could never let anyone know how she really felt about my mother, so she kept both graves in great condition.

I kneeled next to my mother's grave. "Oh, Mom, I don't want to make the wrong decision. I'm so afraid I won't know how to be a good mother to Kayden."

There was the sound of a twig snapping behind me, and I turned my head around in surprise.

Nicole stood there. She was wearing a long, dark coat and fancy fur-lined gray boots, totally unsuitable for walking. I guessed she must have come directly from the salon.

I stood and faced her.

She looked at me expressionlessly. "Mrs. Johnson told me you had rolled into town on your own. I knew you'd be here."

"What is it, Nicole? What is it you want?"

"I want you to help Tiffany."

I stared at her in disbelief. What was it about her and her daughter? They acted so entitled. As if everyone else just existed to do their bidding.

"She's not like you. She's not brave and independent. You're right, I spoiled her too much when she was young. She won't make it in the city. Can't you just take her under your wing? Just help her this once until she finds her own feet. You owe it to her, after you ruined her wedding. She would have gone ahead with marrying Steven and had a nice life if you had not turned up with your shiny new man."

I stayed silent. She did have a point. If I had not turned up, Tiffany would have married Steven and been content with the idea she had stolen my man, taken what I wanted.

"You know, she lost her baby, right?"

"She told me," I said slowly. Just a few weeks ago, I would have told her what Rex told me, but I had grown up a lot since the last time I was here. I no longer wanted Tiffany to seek some petty revenge. I just wanted to heal my old wounds and make myself whole again so I could give the best of myself to Rex and Kayden.

"Please, Willow, I'm begging you."

Whatever I said about Nicole, she did truly love her blood daughters. "All right, I'll help her..."

"Thank you, Willow—"

"I'll help her under one condition."

She stiffened. "What is it?"

"That you answer one question honestly."

Her relief was palpable. "Of course. What is it?"

"Why did you hate me so much? What did I ever do to you to make you hate me the way you do?"

She turned her face away and looked far into the horizon. I watched her take a deep breath before she turned towards me again. "I didn't hate you in the beginning. No, then I thought your father loved me, but very quickly I realized he didn't. He was still in love with your mother. You know, he called her name once, when we were making love. You don't know what that feels like. Competing with a dead woman. Every fucking night she climbed into bed with us.

Oh, how I hated her. And you were a part of her. You even looked like her. Every time he looked at you, you reminded him all over again of her. Every time I looked at you, you reminded me that he did not love me."

She paused for a few seconds.

"Do you understand now?" she cried suddenly. "Do you understand that there was not enough love left for me. You sucked the last bit out of him. I had a dry husk for a husband."

"Thank you. Thank you for being so honest," I whispered.

"So, you'll help Tiffany?"

"You have my word."

She lifted her chin, and looked, suddenly haughty, then she turned and left, the snow crunching under her feet.

The tears began rolling down my cheeks then. I sat at my parents' graves and told them all about Rex and Kayden. My fingers were blue by the time I made it back to the waiting car.

51

WILLOW

I didn't want to be in the suite on my own, so I went to the bar to have a drink. Someone I went to school with was there with some friends, so I joined them. They wanted to hear all about my life in the big city.

But I didn't want to impress them.

What Nicole said still rankled in my head. If not for me and tales of my supposedly glamorous life in the city with my new rich boyfriend, Tiffany would have married Steven. Maybe the relationship wouldn't have lasted, but at least it would have had a chance.

I'd missed lunch and dinner, and two drinks later, I felt so drunk I had to excuse myself and leave. I swayed in the elevator. Incredible how drunk I'd become on two glasses of wine.

Up in the suite, I stumbled across the living area towards the second bedroom and opened the door. It was empty of course, but in my mind I saw him standing at the window looking out at the falling snow. I remembered him turning in the dark to look at me. How unsurprised he had been.

I made it unsteadily over to the window and stood in front of it. It wasn't snowing. That night had been magical. A wave of loneliness hit me, and I missed Rex with an intensity I'd never felt before. I got into my night shirt and slipped into bed with Kayden's soft toy gift and my phone.

My fingers moved.

I miss you.

I hit send and a second later, I saw three dots. Rex was not asleep either. Elation filled me. The feeling of loneliness disappeared.

Rex: I miss you too. Kayden was asking about you today. He was worried you'd gone for good.

Me: Would never happen.

Rex: Shall I call you?

Me: No.

Rex: How was your day?

Me: I'm not sure.

Rex: Tell me what's wrong, babe. Whatever it is, we'll work it out together.

Me: Had too much to drink. Should go to sleep. Big kiss to Kayden. And you.

Rex: Goodnight. I'm here for you.

Me: I know.

I turned off the lights and pulled the covers over my head. God, I loved him so much it hurt. I must be like Jessica. I must put his and Kayden's happiness before my own. No matter what, I'm not going to mess up that poor kid's life.

The tears came then. I cried into my pillow until my head ached and eventually sleep overtook me.

I dreamed of my mother. I was an adult, but she looked

exactly as she had been when I was a child. We were standing on a hill.

"Dad thinks you're dead," I told her.

"Clearly, I'm not," she said, smiling. Then she reached into a suitcase that was lying on the ground and pulled out my blue blouse. It looked as new as the day she had given it to me.

"How is that possible? She ripped it in half, Mom," I cried, surprised.

"A stitch in time saves nine. Nothing is torn forever, my darling," my mother replied.

I woke up then.

I didn't know what the dream meant, but there was a strange peace in my heart. I slid out of bed and walked over to the sliding doors. Opening them I went out onto the balcony. It was freezing cold and dark. The inky black sky was full of bright stars, and it felt as if I was the only person awake in the whole world.

I breathed in the cold air and let it fill my lungs.

So... Nicole hated me because I reminded her that my father still loved my mother. Well, Kayden didn't remind me of Jessica. Not one bit. When I looked at him, I just saw an adorable kid, Rex's kid. Also, I knew for certain Rex didn't love Jessica. She was just a fling to him. I felt no jealousy, nothing, when I thought about her. If anything, I admired her selfless action of making sure her son was in good hands before she passed on.

I thought about little Kayden.

Could I really be a mother to him?

Maybe. Maybe I'll give it a try. If I sucked as a stepmother, I could always walk away then, but at the very least, I should give it a try.

52

WILLOW

https://www.youtube.com/watch?v=YopdQU87dc8

"Willow, it's us," an overly excited little voice said. It sounded so terribly close that I clamped a hand to my mouth to stop myself from crying.

"Kayden?" I whispered.

"Yes," he shouted.

He was close. But it couldn't be.

Then Rex's voice came on. "Willow, we're in the lobby. Hope you're decent because we're coming up."

I jumped out of bed so fast, my head spun. I ran to the bathroom and looked in the mirror. Jesus, I looked like death warmed over. I pulled on the big fluffy robe hanging behind the door while I ran a brush through my hair and swished the hotel's minty blue liquid in my mouth. No time for lip gloss. I pinched my pale cheeks, ran to the door, and flung it open. They were not waiting outside, so I put something to jar the door open and dashed over to the elevator.

Questions swam in my mind. What were they doing here? Why did they come?

Oh my God. I couldn't believe I was going to see that face I dreamed of and longed for all night. I bounced from one foot to another.

The elevator pinged, then opened and they emerged. Kayden ran straight into me, almost knocking me down.

"Kayden," I cried, bending to hug him. "You've grown taller." He really felt as if he had too. I kissed his head over and over again while he twisted restlessly in my arms.

I let go of his squirming body and raised my gaze up to Rex. I swear, I stopped breathing when our gazes met. He had shadows under his eyes. Had he not slept? And yet he looked so ruggedly handsome.

"Hi," I whispered.

Kayden freed himself of my loosening hold and confidently ran into the suite.

"Are you alright?" he asked.

"I am now," I said, standing up. "Come on in."

"Are you sure?" Rex asked, his voice filled with emotion.

I didn't understand what he was asking. "About entering the suite?"

"Yes," he confirmed. "If I enter, I won't leave you. Saying yes means that you want us in your life as much as we want you. I was a fool not to insist on coming with you when I saw clearly you were hurting and shouldn't be alone. I love you, Willow... with every fiber of my being, and I don't want to go one more day without you."

His declaration was so unexpected that it took a few seconds for it to penetrate my brain. When the meaning sunk in, I wanted to jump up and down like a preschooler.

"Do you really mean it?" I asked softly, a feeling of vulnerability coming over me.

"Every word. I love you, Willow. I don't know what's going on with you, but whatever it is we can work it out," Rex said earnestly.

Giddy joy filled me. I took a step forward then threw myself into his arms. Rex wrapped his hands around me.

"I love you too," I cried, holding him as tightly as I could.

"So, you came all this way to find me, huh?" I asked, overwhelmed by emotions.

"That was nothing," Rex said. "I would do it a thousand more times."

I had no idea how long we stayed locked in each other's arms whispering how much we loved each other.

"You haven't answered my question?" Rex said, drawing back to look into my eyes. "Are you sure you want me to enter?"

"Now you're making yourself sound like Dracula," I joked.

"I mean it, Willow. All or nothing."

"All."

He grinned.

But we hadn't entered just yet. I had to kiss Rex to be sure that my mind was not playing cruel tricks on me. I touched his lips with a finger first, trailing it along the outline of his lips. He stayed still as I took in every bit of his face.

Then I went on tip toe and my mouth was on his. So

much was said in that one kiss. I'll never let you go. I'll love you forever. We are a family.

"Willow, Daddy, are you ever coming in?" Kayden moaned, and we were so lost in each other his voice made us jump, then we looked at each other and burst out laughing.

53

WILLOW

https://www.youtube.com/watch?v=1lwDLjO-V7I

"Yeah, we're going tobogganing," Kayden shouted enthusiastically to the other people climbing the gentle slope of the hill with us.

"It's his first time," Rex explained.

They smiled back.

"You're going to love it so much. It's great to feel the wind in your hair," I said.

There were already many people sliding down the snowy slopes as we reached the top.

"You'll go with Daddy," I said.

"No, I'll go with Daddy, then I'll go with you, then I'll go with Daddy, then I'll go with you," Kayden shouted breathlessly in the bracingly cold air.

I laughed. "Okay."

I made sure his helmet was securely on, then I lifted him

and put him between Rex's legs.

"Ready?" Rex asked.

"Ready," he screamed, and off they went. I watched them hurtle down the slope and my heart was so full of love, I thought it would burst.

They came back up. "Quick, Willow. It's our turn together," Kayden said bossily.

I got onto the sled and Rex placed him between my legs. Once I was sure he was secure, we were off. Kayden was screaming with joy and even I couldn't help but laugh at how infectious his joy and exhilaration was.

Suddenly, I heard Rex yelling, his voice urgent and full of panic. My hackles rose as my head swung around. I saw the runaway sled with the teenager sitting inside. His face was white with terror. He was on a collision course with us. There was no time to think. No time to act. He was going to ram into us. There was no way to stop it. All I could do was grab Kayden and hold him tightly with my body as a shield.

The impact when it came was like a crack of thunder. I felt nothing, just a jolt and then Kayden and I were thrown into the air. From that moment on, time ceased to work properly, everything happened as if in slow motion. I held Kayden tightly and let myself take the brunt of the fall. A sharp pain went through my shoulder, but I didn't let go of Kayden. My body slid along the slippery surface. I tried to stop our progress down the hill with my heels, but the momentum was too strong. All I could do was wait for the bottom of the hill. I could hear shouts from the people.

When we got to the bottom, I turned Kayden around to face me and raised him up in the air. His face was white with terror. He stared at me with fear in his eyes.

"Your jacket is torn, Willow," he whispered in a strange,

shocked voice. His face was crumpling, and he looked like he was going to cry.

And in my head, I heard my mother say, "A stitch in time saves nine. Nothing is torn forever, my darling."

I knew what the dream meant. My love for Kayden was the stitch in time, the thing that was going to heal me. I was not going to be torn forever.

I began to laugh.

Watching me laugh made Kayden stop in his intention to cry. He must have thought colliding with another sled and being thrown out of our sled was part of the sport of tobogganing, because a smile trembled onto his lips, then he too began to laugh with me. We were still laughing when Rex and everybody else came to find us.

I looked at Rex's utterly terrified face. "Are you alright?" he asked anxiously, as he gathered Kayden into his arms.

I wiped the tears of joy running down my face. "I may have some bruises or a cracked rib or two, but I've never been better in my life. I know now, I can be a good mother to Kayden."

"What?" he asked, totally bemused by my reply.

"I know now I can put Kayden's safety before mine. Finally, I have proof that I can be a real mother to him," I said happily, even though my back had started to throb with pain.

54

WILLOW

Six Weeks later

I had moved into Rex's condo and let Tiffany have my old apartment. She sniffed when she first came in. I assumed it was some sort of reference to dog smells, but I was pleased to find that her opinion of me or my dog mattered little. I had spent so many years of my life being angry with her.

There was no more anger or frustration in my heart.

When I looked at her now, I felt only pity. I knew she would not make it in New York. She was lazy, narcissistic, undisciplined, talentless, and expected everyone around her to pick up her slack. And you got nowhere with that attitude in a city that never sleeps.

It was dog-eat-dog in the Big Apple.

But she didn't understand that. She had come to New

York with the mistaken idea that wealthy men waiting to become her husband were as common as street lamps.

She even asked me if I would introduce her to one of Rex's rich pals. My reply was short and sharp. I promised her mother I'd help set her up in the city, I never promised to let her ruin Rex's friends' lives.

And ruin them she would too.

So... unless she used her only real asset, her beauty, and found another chump like Steven, who she could manipulate into taking care of her financially, she was undoubtedly going back to Bison Ridge with her tail between her legs.

Looking in the mirror, I touched my ribs and felt no pain. Good. Perhaps now Rex could stop tiptoeing around me and behaving as if I was a piece of china that could break at the slightest touch.

I looked over my jeans and top and decided they were perfect for a casual drop in at his office. I applied a bit of mascara and lipstick then grabbed my purse and headed to the basement parking lot. My heart pounded wildly as I drove towards the office.

I second guessed myself on whether going unannounced was a good idea, but it was always good every time I ambushed him. After inspecting my reflection in the rearview mirror, I got out of the car and strolled in after exchanging pleasantries with the guards. I took the elevator up to the top floor of the building. I stepped out of the elevator, and immediately encountered a security desk I hadn't noticed before.

Hmmm... a lot of changes since I left four weeks ago.

Luckily, I still had my old work badge with me and when I showed it to the uniformed guard, he let me through. The sound of my heels was swallowed by the carpet that lined the hallway. I emerged in a big waiting area manned by a secretary behind a large desk.

She looked up and frowned as if she couldn't place me.

"Hi," I said, moving to stand in front of her desk. "My name is Willow, I'm here to see Rex Hunter." I cleared my throat even though there was nothing obstructing it.

She smiled in that professional, detached way that secretaries did. "Is he expecting you?"

"Yes," I said with as much confidence as I could muster.

She frowned. "He's in a meeting right now. I'll let him know you're here when he's done. He shouldn't be long."

"Fine, I'll just wait until his meeting is over."

"Okay. Make yourself comfortable. Coffee? Soda? Water?" she asked.

If I drank anything I would throw it all up "No thanks." I made my way to a seating area at the corner and chose the furthest seat.

I picked up a magazine from the glass topped table. I had no interest in it but if I sat doing nothing, I'd look like an idiot. Not that his secretary would have noticed. She hadn't looked up from her computer screen from the moment she dismissed me as some floozy chasing her boss.

Half an hour later Rex's meeting had not ended. Grrrrrr...coming to his office had been a mistake. Fifteen minutes later, the door to the inner office opened and two men wearing serious expressions and talking animatedly stepped out with Rex following behind.

He stopped and stared at me. He looked...what was the right word? Intimidating. Maybe it was the suit or the fact that he was in his office. Whatever it was, he wasn't the Rex I see at home.

"Willow, is everything okay?" he asked, striding towards me.

"Of course. I just came to see you."

He leaned in and kissed my cheek which surprised me as well as his secretary who was openly staring at us. "Wait for me in my office. I'm coming." He returned to the two men, and I hurried into his office.

I shut the door and sunk into the visitor's chair to catch my breath. That could have gone very wrong. I needed something to still my pounding heart.

I went to his refrigerator and removed a bottle of wine that was half open. I poured myself a glass and sat down with it. I took a generous sip and sighed as the cool drink went down my throat.

By the time the office door opened, all my tension had ebbed away, and I smiled brightly when Rex entered. He leaned against the door and watched me curiously.

"I see you've already made yourself at home." His tone was teasing.

"I thought that's what you would want."

The corners of his mouth curved in a smile. "Of course."

My heart skipped a beat, and it wasn't because I was nervous. After all this time I still thought Rex was too everything for his own good. Too handsome, too charming, too sexy, too hard to resist. I cleared my throat as I searched for the right words to say what I wanted to say. "I've always had a fantasy."

"Oh yeah?"

"Yeah. I always wanted to fuck a man wearing a blue tie."

He looked down at his tie, then chuckled. "I like this fantasy. Tell me more."

"In my fantasy, he fucks me over the desk."

He started walking towards me.

"He locks the door first," I said.

"Ah," he said, and locked the door. "Then what does this man do?"

"He goes and sits in his chair behind the desk."

Rex lowered himself into his chair while staring at me intently.

I jumped up from my chair and went around to his side of the desk. I swirled his chair around then sank down onto his lap, sitting astride his hips. I threw my hands around his neck.

A tremor of excitement shot through me, and the air changed suddenly as pure need gripped me. Rex's eyes darkened with desire. His hands went around my waist as he pulled me closer so that I was sitting directly on his erection.

Our lips met in a hot, wet slide. Time stopped as our tongues played with each other. All that mattered was the pleasure zipping through me. I threaded my fingers through his hair. Rex's male scent and heat made me dizzy with longing.

I pressed down against his erection, greedy for more friction. Rex's hands caressed my back then moved to raise my blouse. He tore his mouth from mine and brought it down to my breasts. Pulling down the cups of my bra, he took a nipple between his teeth. I bit my lower lip to contain the groan threatening to burst out of me.

"Fuck, Rex," I cried out trying to keep my voice low.

"Is that what you want?" he said and looked up at me, his eyes resembling a brewing storm.

My body ached with need. "Yes. Bend me over the desk."

He frowned. "Your ribs..."

"My ribs are completely healed. Even the doctor said so. If you don't fuck me hard today, I swear, I'm going to think you don't want me."

"Don't want you? Are you crazy? I've been going out of my mind holding back."

"Well, don't. I like the gentle stuff as much as the next girl, but hell, I miss the times when you used to go all wild caveman on me."

He cupped my ass, pressing my pelvis to his erection. Every part of my body was lit with the urgent need to be possessed by Rex.

"Bend over the desk," he ordered suddenly.

A thrill shot through me. Oooo... having sex in an office was all sorts of forbidden and I couldn't wait to cross that off my list.

Behind me, I heard the rustle of clothes, and wanting to feel him inside me as soon as possible, I reached for my jeans.

"I'll do that," Rex growled, and I returned my hands to their earlier position on the desk.

His hands unbuttoned, then zipped down my jeans, before gripping the hems of my jeans and yanking them down. Playfully, I wiggled my hips as the jeans went down, and he smacked my bottom. I gasped at the sting. He ripped my panties off. My pussy throbbed and ached for him.

Rex spread my thighs wider. "Are you wet?"

"I am."

He ran a lone finger up and down my slit, spreading my slickness, and I arched my back, exposing more of myself to him. My breath came out in gasps even though Rex was merely touching me with a finger. Anticipation was making me feverish.

"Go on, Rex. Take me," I urged, unable to bear the torture any longer.

He cursed under his breath in response. Then I felt what I needed the most. The tip of his cock pushing into my slick pussy. A long, drawn-out moan left my mouth as he went in deeper and deeper. Sweat formed on my face. I parted my lips to get enough air into my lungs.

Rex gripped my hips with both hands and pulled out his cock until only the tip remained buried in me.

"Fuck me, Rex," I urged him.

He groaned and slammed into me, propelling me to new heights of pleasure with every thrust. I tried to keep my voice low, afraid that his secretary would hear. A moment later, I didn't care whether everyone in the whole building heard us. All I cared about was chasing the orgasm swirling in my core.

It didn't take long.

In less than three minutes, I was gripping Rex's desk as an orgasm sent my body shaking and my brain reeling.

"Oh God," I cried out over and over again.

Rex growled and slammed into me harder as he came, whispering sweet, meaningless words into my ear. When it was over, he leaned over and peppered my back with kisses. It was a tender gesture.

He pulled me up gently from where I lay sprawled on the desk and turned me around. He stared into my eyes.

"Was I too rough? Are you okay?" he asked.

"No. You were perfect. Just perfect, man with the blue tie," I said with a slow smile.

He smiled back. "I should make a habit of wearing a blue tie."

"You should." Then I laughed... with sheer happiness.

55

REX

Six months Later

I woke up to the scent of Willow, strong, sweet and tantalizing. I opened my eyes to the sight of her sprawled beside me on the bed. Naked. At least her shoulders were. She stirred and turned around to face me. Yeah. She was definitely naked.

"Did we have sex?"

She grinned. "Definitely not. What we did was down a lot of shots."

Willow hit me with a pillow. "Your relief is not flattering."

"Relief because I thought we had sex, and I couldn't remember." I pulled her to lie on top of me. My erection pressed against her pelvis. "Is this flattering though, Willow Tree?"

The laughter in her mouth died, and her eyes took on a deeper shade of green.

"Who would we hurt if we have sex one last time, as two single people?"

"No one," I whispered.

The image of my cock sheathed inside her pussy walls was already throbbing in my head. It never failed to amaze me how desperately I always wanted her. No matter how many times we did it, I craved more.

"Well, hurry up then. I have to slip back into my room and act all chaste when your mother comes to help me get into my dress."

I get to work immediately. I made sure to put the color into the bride's cheeks.

EPILOGUE

WILLOW

Two years later

"Shall we serve dinner now?" Martin, our chef asked. "Everything is ready."

My stomach rumbled at the tantalizing smells that came from the kitchen. I wished I could stuff myself, but these days I filled up first. Maybe it was because the baby was taking up so much space and leaving little for food. This was going to be our first Christmas back home after a year of living in California, where Rex was setting up a business.

It had been a magical year. So much had happened. Rex and I had gotten married, a small ceremony with just Matt as his best man, Emma as my maid of honor, Alice, Olivia, Caroline, his parents, and some of our friends. I didn't invite Tiffany or Nicole. It seemed pointless. It would have eaten them up with jealousy and they would have tried to spoil my wedding day.

"I'll let everyone know," I said and moved to the living room where everyone had gathered.

Pogo was asleep on Shadow's stomach. I slipped my hand around Rex's waist, and he held me close and rested one hand on my belly. I swear my husband loved my pregnant belly more than my normal one.

"Dinner is ready," I called, drawing everyone's attention.

"I'll go get the boys," Alice said, referring to her little boy and our Kayden. They were in the playroom.

"Good luck," I said, knowing that they would beg her to eat in the playroom.

She laughed. "I have a few bribes up my sleeve."

The rest of us moved to the dining room. We sat around the table and held hands to say a blessing over the food. As Alice said the blessing, Rex and I met gazes.

"I love you so much," he mouthed.

My heart expanded filling every space in my chest. "I love you so much too."

TIFFANY

https://www.youtube.com/watch?v=jYa1eI1hpDE&

I heard the key in the door and immediately I straightened my clothes a bit. I'd been drinking vodka and lounging on the couch watching television all day.

Mom hated that. She thought I was wasting my life away.

Yeah, I guess I was, but she didn't understand that there was nothing for me to live for anymore. My dreams were all ashes in my mouth. I lived a life of regret. I know I'd fucked up big time. I could see clearly now that in every situation I'd gone and made the wrong choice, done the wrong thing.

I no longer liked life.

Plus...

She didn't know what really happened to me in New York.

How a man I met at a bar lured me to a secret party that he claimed would be crammed full of the richest men on earth. I was so excited. I couldn't believe my luck. Here was my chance. I'd show Willow I could bag myself a rich man too.

It was true they were all insanely rich, some of them had flown in from Dubai specially for the party, but they were perverted rich men.

I was drugged and used all night long as if I was a piece of meat. So many men entered me. Roughly, they entered all my orifices. None of them used a condom. They filled me with their cum. There was so much cum, it seeped from my mouth, my sex, and my ass. When I vomited later, I vomited cum. It was the most horrible taste.

I wanted to scream, but I couldn't. My mouth was frozen.

But they knew I was suffering because tears ran out of the sides of my eyes the whole time. I think they liked seeing me cry because they laughed. Their faces were a blur. They were like children. They pressed, they pinched, they prodded, they bit, they even took me to a bathroom and pissed on me.

I felt like a toilet.

By the time they were all finished I was bleeding badly. The man who took me to the party dropped me off at my apartment.

"You'll be all right in a few days," he said, and after putting a couple of hundred dollars next to me he left.

I never saw him again.

In the cold light of the morning, I stood in front of the mirror, and I couldn't believe my eyes. There was not an inch on my body that was not blue and black with bruises. I couldn't walk straight for days.

I let the most obvious bruises heal before I fled from New York and went back to Bison Ridge.

Everybody wondered why I'd come back. I told them

New York was overrated. I would never tell anyone what those men had done to me. How they had used me.

Of course, I was never the same.

While I was at the salon yesterday, I'd learned that Steven was getting married. It hurt to hear that. Once he had loved me and I had thrown it away. I hated to admit it, but I deeply regretted what I did. I should have married him. Then New York and those terrible men would never have happened.

I would never have become the sad drunk I am now.

"Hi, honey," my mom said.

"Hi Mom," I replied, trying not to slur my words.

"Have you been sitting there all day?"

"Leave me alone, Mom."

"Honey, I'm just worried about you."

"Yeah. Well don't. I'm fine."

"You're not. You sit in front of the TV all day long drinking. It's not healthy, Tiff. You're a young woman. You have your whole life to live."

"For heaven's sake, leave me the fuck alone."

"Stop swearing. I can't leave you alone, Tiff. You're ruining your life."

"Do you still have Steven's number, Mom?"

"Why?"

"I just thought I'd call and congratulate him. He's getting married, isn't he?"

"He is."

"Well, do you have his number?"

"Yes, I have his number, but you can't call him, Tiff. He's got a kid with that woman."

I got to my feet unsteadily. "Give me his number," I screamed.

My mother did what she always did, she gave in to my tantrum and gave me his number. Maybe that's why I hated her so much.

Maybe I would call him. After all, he was mine first.

Maybe tomorrow. Tomorrow, I will make the first right decision for the first time in my life.

The End.

COMING NEXT - SAMPLE CHAPTERS

BOSS FROM HELL

Chapter One
Lillian

"I don't understand why he won't just pop the question," Maggie wondered in a frustrated voice, a hand rubbing the back of her neck. "I'm not fussy. I don't need anything fancy. Hell, he could ask me to marry him on a bus and I'd happily say yes."

I wanted to laugh at the image that popped into my mind, but I didn't. Maggie's pain was real. I covered her hand with mine. "He's probably just taking his time to be sure. You're the one who is always complaining about how long he takes to make a decision."

It was the wrong thing to say. Maggie's features became pinched. "We've known each other for seven years. What is he still unsure about?"

"I don't know. Maybe he wants it to be perfect. Why not relax and enjoy the ride?"

"Easy for you to say," she muttered, and drained half her cocktail.

An idea dropped into my head. "Why don't you propose to him?"

I had to laugh at the expression of horror on her face. "I can't do that. I'll look desperate."

"You are desperate," I pointed out.

"I'm not," she denied vehemently.

"You are. Be honest. You can't wait to start your own home and have a family, can you?"

That had been my dream too, once upon a time. But life had flipped things around for me, and now I was just focused on surviving day to day. There was no time for dreams anymore when real life was so tough and demanding.

Maggie nodded. "Fine, I'll give you that, but there's no way I'm ever proposing to a man. Anyway, enough about me." She leaned forward, her eyes shining. "Tell me what's going on with you."

Maggie had a talent for flipping her mood around. She could be down and out one moment and the next, she could be laughing uproariously as if she didn't have a care in the world. I knew her well. We've been friends since we met in third grade after her family moved to New York.

"Well..." I said, and paused. Where to start with the mess my life was in?

"Start with the job hunt. How's that going?" she prompted.

"It's not going," I admitted, and sipped my chardonnay.

"Why is that then?"

"I don't know. I've sent several resumes, but so far...

nothing. Sometimes it feels as if I'm sending them into the ether to disappear forever."

Maggie frowned. "That's strange. You're good at your job. and you have excellent references."

"To be honest, I'm getting a little worried. I have savings, of course, but my monthly expenses are high, and I could eat through it in no time. I need a job sooner rather than later."

"Hmmm... actually I have an opening at the agency that I could hook you up with. It pays really well."

I brightened. "You have?"

She shook her head while making a face. "Nah, what am I thinking of? That's not you at all. Forget it."

"Don't do that. Tell me more."

"Trust me when I tell you that job is more trouble than it's worth."

"No, tell me about it and let me decide," I urged.

"Well, I suppose, if you're really, really desperate..."

"I am really, really desperate," I said quickly. "Please, tell me about it."

"It's PA to a ghastly man called Maximus Frost."

"Who is he?" I asked.

"He owns Frost Investments and I suppose it's actually a very well-paid job with awesome bonuses. She told me the figure and I gasped.

"Yeah," she said. "That's how much no one wants to work for him. It's more of a bribe than a salary because the man is a tyrant. An absolute monster. The phrase, 'boss from hell' was invented to describe him. I swear he's been through more secretaries than any CEO in the past 100 years. I keep sending my girls to him and he keeps sending them back."

"Wow."

"Yeah, he has a reputation of being a complete asshole. No PA has lasted even a full month."

I was intrigued. "Maybe I would."

She shook her head. "You wouldn't. We've sent all our best people and they all leave that job in the first if not second week."

"I think I'd like to try."

She laughed, her eyes twinkling like blue stars in her face. "Sure, if you want to give it a shot, be my guest. In fact, I'll even make it a little bit more interesting and throw in a hundred dollars if you can last more than a month."

I laughed in disbelief. "You betting on me not lasting a month?"

"That's right."

I looked at her with narrowed eyes. "Are you serious?"

"Dead serious. I'm happy to lose a hundred bucks if I can send someone to him that he'll keep for longer than a month."

"You're on," I said. "One hundred bucks says I can stay the whole month."

She shook her head. "You really can't resist a bet, can you?"

"And the salary," I quipped.

She grinned and drowned the rest of her cocktail. "Looks like I just won myself a hundred dollars because the job is yours. I'll email you the details.

I sipped my wine and enjoyed the feeling of the cold liquid going down my throat, and warned, "Don't count your chickens before they're laid."

"Oh, I'm pretty sure these chicks are getting laid," she claimed confidently.

"Tell me more about him," I invited.

She told me about how he came from a ridiculously wealthy family, but had built his own multi-billion-dollar company from scratch. His investment company was one of the leading investment firms in the country.

"That's why his attitude puzzles me," Maggie said. "He behaves like a spoiled brat which he isn't considering how hard he has worked to get where he is."

"I think I'll be able to handle Mr. Frost."

"Just don't be shocked if you're out of there in a week," she warned darkly. "You won't be the first or the last."

I raised my glass. "That is not going to happen. I have a way with bosses... and I've had my share of difficult ones."

She clinked her empty glass with mine, then summoned the waiter for another round. I wasn't worried about Mr. Frost. My responsibilities made it irrelevant how my boss behaved. The bottom line was what mattered and that was being able to make my mother's mortgage payments on time.

She ordered another round of drinks, then turned back to me. Her eyes were gleaming. "Oh by the way, I forgot to mention. Maximus Frost, by all accounts, is sex on a stick."

She laughed at my shocked expression. "Good luck, winning the bet."

Chapter Two
Lillian

I usually spent most Sunday mornings at my mother's house helping her with her weekly cleaning. That Sunday was no different and not for the first time, I thought she should sell the house and buy something smaller. We were dusting the upstairs guest bedroom.

"Um... how are your finances, sweetheart?" mom asked casually as she dusted a picture frame of my dad that rested on the night table.

Ever since Henry, my stepfather, passed on, my father's photographs appeared all over the house. As if she wanted to forget that she'd had a second husband. I didn't blame her. Henry had messed up her life big time.

She tried to make the question about job hunting sound casual, but I could hear the worry in her voice.

"Not too bad," I replied, my voice equally casual.

"I was thinking," she said, straightening up to look at me. "Why don't you move back home."

She saw the expression of dismay on my face and smiled. "Lillian, it will help you cut down on expenses. Besides, you should be here. After all, you shoulder most of the mortgage burden."

"Don't say that."

"It's true," she said. "And I'm more than grateful for it." Her lower lip started trembling and she bit down on it.

I sighed. It probably wasn't the best time to bring up selling the house and moving to a smaller place. There was no reason for her to live in a five-bedroom house. The mortgage was expensive and if she sold it, she could pay it off and buy something smaller outright.

"It's fine, honestly. You know I'm happy to do it, and I'm starting a job on Monday."

Helping her with the mortgage payments was nothing compared to the horror we had lived through when the receivers had come and the restaurant was gone.

I shook my head free of those memories. I was determined to forge ahead with life and not focus on the things that had gone wrong. Moving back home was a recurring nightmare and I had no intention of making it a reality.

"A job?" she asked, perking up.

"It's only temporary."

"Oh well, the offer still stands."

"Thanks Mom, but you know me. I love my space."

"I know," she said and patted my hand with affection. "You've always been so independent. Much more than Rose." She frowned. "Have you spoken to your sister lately?"

"I spoke to her yesterday. She's fine, and so are the girls and Dylan," I said.

We moved our cleaning stuff to the next room.

"Did she say anything about getting a job?" my mother asked.

That was her and Rose's bone of contention. Their conversations frequently ended in shouting matches with Rose accusing Mom of making her out to be lazy. Rose and Dylan had decided that she would stay home until the twins went to school, but that didn't sit well with Mom.

"You know the answer to that," I told her gently as I wiped down the desk.

"A woman should have something of her own," Mom grumbled. "You never know when things can change."

I hated my stepfather for the mess he had left for my mother to clean up. It had been his dream to own a sports bar and grill and he had convinced my mom to join him on the enterprise. She had left her job, remortgaged the house, and taken out a loan at the bank.

It had seemed to work at first but it soon became apparent that the ship was sinking. After the initial excitement of a new restaurant, the dinner crowd had thinned and Mom had taken another loan without our knowledge, to service the other loan. Madness.

"Dylan earns enough now, but he could lose his job," she continued.

Mom had always been an optimistic person. That was the reason why Henry had managed to convince her to hop on his dream. But these days, she saw the glass as half empty, and who could blame her after the financial wringing she had gone through.

"He's not going to lose his job," I said. "And even if he did, dentists are in high demand in New York, everyone wants to have a brilliant smile."

She smiled and relaxed. "That is true. So tell me about this temporary job."

I told her about Maximus Frost and his reputation for being a difficult boss. I'd have told my "old mom" about the bet, and she would probably have wanted in on the fun, but not now. It would piss her off that we were taking life so casually by betting on something as important as a job.

It saddened me to see her worry about everything. Life had become precarious for her.

After spending the morning cleaning the house, I made a salad and we sat down to eat lunch together. She regaled me with harmless gossip from the doctor's office where she worked as an assistant. More than helping with the mortgage, the job kept her busy enough so that when she came home in the evenings, she didn't dwell too much on what she had lost.

I left after lunch and headed to the farmer's market to buy veggies for the next weeks' dinner as I'd be at work, working for Maximus Frost.

Chapter Three
Max

"Your coffee Sir," the waiter said and placed, a cup of steaming black liquid before me.

I grunted a response and took a sip. It was my third cup of the day and it was only nine in the morning. Next week I planned to reduce it, to a maximum of two cups a day.

"What did you think?" Chris, my Head of Research asked. "The two guys weren't the most compelling marketers, but if their product works the way they say it could..."

We'd spent the morning listening to a pitch from two young men who were developing a mobile app that enabled users to send and receive money faster and cheaper than PayPal or any other competitor. While it was in the developmental phase and a long way from beta, I was definitely interested.

"Agree. Great idea, but niggling worries about their ability to execute," I said, and for the next twenty minutes we discussed the idea and how much we needed to invest in it, if we did go ahead.

Afterwards, we took the short walk back to our offices. Chris got off the elevator on his floor and I went up one further. The security guard who manned my floor called out a morning greeting. I ignored him and headed straight to my office. After all this time, he still didn't get it. His job was not to brown nose me. His job was to guard the premises.

I ground to a halt at the sight of a woman sitting at the desk in my outer office.

"Who the fuck are you?" I barked.

She looked, her wide blue eyes as calm as a blue lake on a hot summer day, and fucking smiled at me. She grated on me before she even opened her mouth to speak.

Standing up, she straightened her pencil skirt as if I had all day to wait for her. "Good morning, Mr. Frost. My name is—"

"I didn't ask your name. I asked you what the fuck you are doing here." I snapped, cutting her off. I wasn't interested in what her name was.

"I'm your new personal assistant," she said, that eerily calm smile never leaving her face.

Robotically calm women gave me the creeps. I narrowed my eyes as I jogged my memory. I didn't remember the temp agency emailing to let me know that they would send someone. Oh well, it didn't matter. I stared her up and down. She was quite something in the looks department, but if she thought her sex appeal would cut it here, she had another thing coming. True I had a thing for women in tight pencil skirts, but only in totally different circumstances. When I was at work, I was in purely work mode.

"Fine. Get me a coffee. black, no sugar," I turned to go to my office, then I remembered I was cutting down on coffee. "No, don't. Get me some water. None of that plastic stuff, make sure it's in a bottle. I have a running account at the deli down the street." I entered my office and deliberately banged the door shut behind me.

I turned on my computer and logged onto my email account. Without a personal assistant, my inbox was flooded with emails. I scrolled through, opening important ones and responding with brief replies where necessary. I lost myself in my work and when a knock came on my door, I looked up with no small amount of irritation.

"Come in," I thundered.

The door swung open and Miss what's-her-name strolled in. "Your water, Mr. Frost."

A crack sounded from the back of my neck. I'd been sitting in the same position for too long. I massaged the source of the pain and looked at my new PA properly for the first time. She was actually quite ravishing, with lustrous long blonde hair tightly held back in a ponytail.

A heart shaped face, plump lips, but those eerily blank blue eyes. Imagine fucking that! My gaze dropped down to her tight skirt. She had curves, if you liked that sort of thing.

I did, but not at work.

I made a mental guess of how long she would last. Probably less than a week. Despite her nice packaging, they were all the same. Inefficient. They expected special treatment as if it was my job to make it nice and comfortable for them, when they fucked up.

I raised my gaze and met her cool one, staring right back at me. Another woman would have reacted to my shameless examination in two ways. One was embarrassment and the other was pride, thrusting out her chin and posing like a model.

My new PA did neither. She waited for me to finish my inspection. Her non-reaction, and those eyes that should have creeped me out, did something different to me. They made me want to fuck her. Right there on my desk. I wanted to bend her over my desk, bunch the pencil skirt around her waist, and give her the riding she deserved. I wanted to see that lake ripple with lust.

Heat whipped through me and rushed to my cock.

What the-?

I'd never had such a violent reaction to any of my personal assistants. I preferred my women to be willing, anonymous hook-ups.

"What's your name?"

"Lillian Hudson," she said calmly.

My cock swelled even more. Never mind, she would probably be gone by the end of the week, anyway. Which, the way things were shaping up would be a good outcome. Might as well hasten her departure with some unreasonable requests.

"Make sure HR sorts out an email for you," I said, and opening the top drawer of my desk I pulled out a file. I'd had so many assistants over the last two years that I'd had a special binder made to give them a crash course in what they needed to work for me.

You'd think that being handed all the instructions in one place would make it a breeze, but they were all idiots. I had the bad luck of getting saddled with fools who didn't know how to do their work.

"Read that," I said to her.

Then I pulled out another folder and handed it to her. It contained projected numbers and calculations that I needed fed into my database. Okay. Maybe I didn't need the whole thing done, but I wanted to see how calm and collected Lillian Hudson would be after hours of heavy, monotonous work.

Would she think she was too big for data entry and quit today? If she was a quitter, better still. I didn't quite like that she was so distracting. I'd rather she left so I could get back to things the way they were before she arrived. I wanted to go back to thinking with my brain.

I told her what to do and curtly dismissed her.

She didn't make a move to leave, but she did flip through the folder. A frown pulled at her very kissable lips. "All this?" she asked quietly. "You want it *all* done today?"

I swung a black look at her. "Is that a problem?"

Her facial muscles moved and produced that supercilious smile. "Not at all, Mr. Frost."

"Anything else I can help you with?" I asked sarcastically.

"No, Sir," she said crisply, turned and left.

For some reason, I felt a pull of something approaching compassion. Something I had not felt in a long time. I pushed it away and focused on my work. I only had an hour to clear my inbox, then I had two client meetings, back to back, then lunch with a potential client.

It was blissfully quiet as I usually had any phone calls rerouted to the switchboard until eleven. That gave me peace to get some work done during the morning hours. I read through some proposals from our managers, then made some calls after deciding on what sounded interesting.

My cell phone broke the blissful silence in the room. I glanced at the screen and almost groaned. It was my mother. Was she in town? I hoped not. I swiped the screen.

"Hello Mother," I said, barely containing my impatience.

"Hello Maximus," she said in her deeper than normal voice. She was the only one who insisted on using my tediously pretentious full name. "You haven't called in almost two weeks. Don't you miss your parents?"

I quelled the rising irritation. "Mother, we spoke a week ago." My mother had a selective memory when she wanted to.

"I miss my only child," she said.

I settled back and scrolled through a business proposal while she prattled through a list of complaints. They started with me and things I had, or hadn't done, then moved to my father and how he wasn't being attentive to her needs.

My mother was one reason I'd been eager to leave Connecticut. She was needy and clingy and it drove me crazy. It wasn't quite as grating on the phone as in person.

"I'm in New York and I've booked a table at the Four Seasons for three at eight o'clock," she said.

I stopped reading. My head jerked up. Shit. All that time, she had been working up to tell me that. It was just like her to just show up without letting me know in advance she was coming.

"You're in New York?"

"Yes, but don't fall over yourself with excitement."

The next worse thing after her neediness was her sarcasm.

"You should have let me know you were coming," I said, barely able to keep the irritation out of my voice.

"I will. Next time," she said breezily.

"You said you made reservations for three. Who is joining us?" I asked.

"Bring your girlfriend. You can't tell me there's no one in your life Maximus."

"There isn't," I said, gritting my teeth. My mother meddling in my love life was the third reason she was so annoying.

"Fine. Come alone, but if you change your mind..."

"See you later," I said, and cut the connection.

I had five minutes to spare before the client meeting. Needing to stretch, I got up and left my office. Lillian was at her desk, her brow faintly creased as she concentrated on something that didn't look like the work I'd given her to do.

"Have you started on inputting the numbers I gave you?"

"No Sir, I haven't. I thought it wiser to read the other file you gave me first."

"Why do I always get the lazy ones?" I muttered, exasperated.

She gazed back, completely unruffled.

"Show the clients in when they come," I ordered, and walked away in disgust.

"Yes, Sir."

My clients arrived a few minutes later. Lillian showed them in and offered them drinks. I had to admit that she was cool and professional, and no one could have guessed it was her first day. In the afternoon, she knocked on my office door and when I barked at her to enter, she did so with that annoyingly tranquil smile fixed on her face.

I found my eyes raking over her body. What the fuck was wrong with me? Sure, she had a smoking hot body, but I didn't hit on employees. Ever. It was a hard rule. No negotiations.

"All done," she announced maddeningly.

"What is all done?" I snapped.

"The data you gave me to enter into your database. It's done."

Impossible. I frowned darkly at her. "All of it?"

The deliberately blank smile widened slightly. I recognized it. She was feeling victorious. "All of it. I found a way to do it in batch form."

I had to see that for myself. I clicked on the mouse until it took me to the custom-made program that enabled me to see our numbers at a glance. She wasn't lying. She had done it.

A new respect for her came over me. Maybe she wasn't as pathetic as the rest of them. I looked up and nodded curtly, and dismissed her with a wave of my hand. Dismissing her from my mind was a bit harder as I continued reading a report about one of our potential clients.

I left my office at half past five and Lillian was still at her desk.

"Good night, Sir."

"I need you to accompany me to dinner," I said brusquely.

"Sorry?"

"You didn't think this was a nine to five job, did you?"

"No, Sir," she said serenely. "Which file do I need to take with me?"

"The White Water one."

She could keep my mother company while I worked on that file.

ABOUT THE AUTHOR

If you wish to leave a review for this book
please do so here:
Heat Of The Moment

Please click on this link to receive news of my latest releases
and great giveaways.
http://bit.ly/10e9WdE

and remember
I **LOVE** hearing from readers so by all means come and say
hello here:

ALSO BY GEORGIA LECARRE

Owned

42 Days

Besotted

Seduce Me

Love's Sacrifice

Masquerade

Pretty Wicked (novella)

Disfigured Love

Hypnotized

Crystal Jake 1,2&3

Sexy Beast

Wounded Beast

Beautiful Beast

Dirty Aristocrat

You Don't Own Me 1 & 2

You Don't Know Me

Blind Reader Wanted

Redemption

The Heir

Blackmailed By The Beast

Submitting To The Billionaire

The Bad Boy Wants Me

Nanny & The Beast

His Frozen Heart

The Man In The Mirror

A Kiss Stolen

Can't Let Her Go

Highest Bidder

Saving Della Ray

Nice Day For A White Wedding

With This Ring

With This Secret

Saint & Sinner

Bodyguard Beast

Beauty & The Beast

The Other Side of Midnight

The Russian Billionaire

CEO's Revenge

Mine To Possess

Printed in Great Britain
by Amazon